Am I the Last Virgin?

Ten African American Reflections on Sex and Love

Am I the Last Virgin?

Ten African American Reflections on Sex and Love

Edited by Tara Roberts

SIMON & SCHUSTER BOOKS FOR YOUNG READERS

SIMON & SCHUSTER BOOKS FOR YOUNG READERS
An imprint of Simon & Schuster Children's Publishing Division
1230 Avenue of the Americas, New York, New York 10020
Am I the Last Virgin? © 1997 by Tara Roberts
House Arrest © 1997 by Tayari Jones
A Bond of Love © 1997 by Corliss Hill
MammaSea and Me © 1997 by Anasuya Isaacs
The Menstrual Hut © 1997 by Eisa Nefertari Ulen
My Trip Down Celebrity Lane © 1997 by Lisa Chestnut-Chapman
Breaking the Silence © 1997 by Kim-Monique Johnson
Moved to Strength © 1997 by Taiia Sojourner Smart
Quilt of Comfort © 1997 by Chemin Abner-Ware
Loving Arms © 1997 by Calinda N. Lee
Simon & Schuster Books for Young Readers is
a trademark of Simon & Schuster.
Book design by Symon Chow
The text for this book is set in Apollo MT.
Printed and bound in the United States of America
First edition
10 9 8 7 6 5 4 3 2 1
Also available in an Aladdin Paperbacks edition.

Library of Congress Cataloging-in-Publication Data
Am I the last virgin? : Ten African American reflections on sex and love / edited
by Tara Roberts. — 1st ed.
       p.   cm.
Summary: A collection of essays discussing issues surrounding the sexual
coming-of-age experiences of African American women.
1. Afro-American teenage girls—Sexual behavior—Juvenile literature.
2. Afro-American teenage girls—Psychology—Juvenile literature.
3. Afro-American teenage girls—Abuse of—Juvenile literature.
[1. Teenage girls—Sexual behavior. 2. Afro-Americans—Sexual behavior.
3. Interpersonal relations. 4. Conduct of life.]
I. Roberts, Tara.
HQ27.5.A45   1997   306.7'0835'2—dc20   96-23793   CIP   AC
ISBN 0-689-80449-0

Contents

Introduction 1

Am I the Last Virgin? 5
Who cares if everyone else is doing it? This young woman isn't giving in to peer pressure.
by Tara Roberts

House Arrest 12
After being raped by a stranger in her neighborhood, a young woman overcomes her fear of leaving the house.
by Tayari Jones

A Bond of Love 22
She never thought sex would be the issue that put her friendship with her mother to the test.
by Corliss Hill

MammaSea and Me 27
A mythical underwater "spirit guide" helps a child heal from the wounds of sexual abuse.
by Anasuya Isaacs

The Menstrual Hut 35
Carrying on the tradition of women from ancient African cultures, a young writer surrounds herself with a strong circle of women.
by Eisa Nefertari Ulen

My Trip Down Celebrity Lane 41
The brother was *fine*, and she gave herself to him — heart and
soul. The hardest part was getting herself back.
by Lisa Chestnut-Chapman

Breaking the Silence 49
She keeps telling herself that she couldn't be gay, but every time
she's around her best friend, her heart tells her differently.
by Kim-Monique Johnson

Moved to Strength 55
Black, unwed, pregnant. Would she become another statistic?
by Taiia Sojourner Smart

Quilt of Comfort 61
She thought AIDS happened to *other* people.
by Chemin Abner-Ware

Loving Arms 68
Healing from incest is painful, but worth it.
by Calinda N. Lee

Resource Directory 73
Compiled by Joyce E. Davis

Authors' Biographies 101

This book is dedicated to the
positive sexual expression of
young adult black women.
—T. R.

Acknowledgments

Thanks eternally to Todd Williams for the idea of turning my "Am I the Last Virgin?" essay into a book—without that bug, none of this would have been possible; the *Essence* staff, particularly editor-in-chief Susan L. Taylor, Valerie Wilson Wesley, Linda Villarosa, Diane Weathers, Gordon Chambers, and co-editor and friend for life Corliss Hill for their many different levels of support and belief in me and my abilities; Stephanie Stokes Oliver, editor-in-chief of *Heart and Soul,* for seeing me as an *Essence* woman before I saw it myself; Andrea Davis Pinkney, my editor, who saw the value in this idea and pushed it through the cracks; Landmark Education for calling forth in me a possibility from which this book could stand; Sheryl Wright, Lucinda Holt, Karima Grant, and Anastasia Rowland for the daily and Saturday sista-support sessions full of love and gentle pushing; the contributors to the book for their courage and willingness to share personal triumphs and struggles and not worry about what the rest of the world will say; and finally to my Mom for EVERY-THING, especially her attempts to raise a sexually happy and healthy whole young adult. I love you.

Introduction

This book is about sexual strength, an infallible strength that exists within ten black women—friends and powerful sisters who have taken control of the sexual images and ideas being produced about them, and agreed to share them. With stories ranging from incest memories to coping with AIDS to my own story of virginity, we all affirm ourselves and our sexual choices and provide insight and life-affirming views of the sexual coming-of-age experience.

Unfortunately not all young-adult black women claim positive experiences. Many remain confused about their bodies, uncertain about their roles in relationships, and in doubt about ways to empower themselves against sexually charged life-threatening situations. This lack of discussion threatens the very fabric of young women's lives. The statistics speak for themselves. According to a report issued by the Children's Defense Fund, every 65 seconds a black teenager becomes sexually active; every 104 seconds a black teenage girl becomes pregnant; every 20 hours a black child or young adult under age 25 dies from causes related to HIV. The Center for Policy Studies reports that black women are almost twice as likely to be raped as white women.

This is one of the first times a collective of young black women has come together to share their sexual stories. These women represent the mass. They are next-door neighbors, school-mates in your math class, colleagues with the same job frustrations. These instantly recognizable women reach deep in their hearts and offer up their hard-earned lessons. If they can make it, they say, so can you.

Read this book at night in bed, with only the comfort of your covers and a flashlight, so you can laugh, cry, and know you're not alone in this struggle. Hear young sisters speaking out strongly and firmly with folded arms and shining eyes about their choices and their lives. Some have navigated through murky waters, but all have emerged into a warmth that requires strength and calls forth the power from within. I hope this book breaks down the barriers and loosens our otherwise tight tongues to begin a dialogue. Black girls have to know they have alliances and people who believe in who they are so they can grow up safe and secure and sexually happy. As sisters we must share the stories, the pain, the joy, the sadness, and the laughter. Only then will we build bridges for those still struggling to make it home to their strength.

—Tara Roberts

Am I the Last Virgin?

Ten African American Reflections
on Sex and Love

Am I the Last Virgin?

by Tara Roberts

In part it was watching music videos and seeing the images of scantily clad female "bootays" shaking and jiggling to the beats of some man's song that strengthened my reserve. As did observing the faceless women being pimped across the screen according to some brother's understanding of their sexuality. It was also attempting to ease the late-night, teary-eyed phone sessions of sisters wondering why their man wasn't acting right and how they were going to fix that slut he was cheating with. But ultimately, I think, it was listening to the sweet-talking lips of brothers themselves that did it for me.

Their refusal to uphold visions of female sexuality that were about more than just "getting some" made me decide early on that I wanted to be in control of and empowered by my sexuality. I did not want to be involved with anyone who could not re-enforce the positive, life-affirming image I had constructed of myself. These brothers weren't "dogs"; they were just like all of us in high school—sisters included—working through their own insecurities, and, unfortunately, buying into stereotypical negative notions of maleness.

Thus I chose, and still am choosing, virginity.

For me, the introduction into the sensual world began early. I remember at my first house parties the music pounding continuously, the repetitive raw bass and drum lines booming over and over again as we kids sweated and gyrated against walls and in corners to the unrelenting beat. The music taught sensuality without intercourse; it forced us to concentrate on expressing, through dance moves, the way the music made us feel. Whenever I walked into one of those hot, dark, crowded dance halls, I could feel the intensity and connectedness in the air. Alliances with people I'd never see again were solidified through the music in this otherworldly place. It was glorious—divine.

But slowly that changed. I started hanging out at clubs and pay-parties, trying to be cool and hip like most kids in high school. But instead of the free and easy sensual exploration I loved so much from the old parties in the 'hood, the music and the moves now seemed more cold, more razor-sharp, more impersonal. Even though I felt pressure to join the fast-swelling ranks of those who were "doing it," something about the way we were behaving scared me. For protection I tried to close off the sexual part of myself.

It wasn't until college that I began struggling with my choice again. And with the increasing urges from my body, I finally decided it was ridiculous for me to still be a virgin.

So one summer, I went to the Motherland and met a fly Zimbabwean brother with big brown eyes and more pairs of Nikes and baggy jeans than I'd ever seen. He was sweet and attentive, and could cut some crazy cool moves on the dance floor. He was the original bad boy on the Continent, coining the phrase "Gee" before I'd ever heard it, and rolling blunts with the quickness and efficiency of a pro. And he thought I was the greatest: he loved my sophistication, my "straight, straight" hair, my grace, and especially the fact that my white clothing always stayed white in his dusty land. I was his African American princess. And on my last day in the country, I was feeling a little melancholy. I wanted a big story to tell my girlfriends at home over lunch. I asked myself, "What could be a better ending

❀

to a trip to the Motherland than making love to my own personal African God?"

My prince's kisses had always been a little too wet and sloppy. And he was a little selfish whenever we got into heavier petting. But he was cute. And so that last night I decided I was ready. As we danced in our usual spot, the swirling lights caressed me. A slow sensuous groove pumped over the loud speakers. I pulled him close and whispered in his ear, "Let's do it."

We rushed back to his place, and with a little foreplay, he whipped it out and went straight for the gusto. I tried to slow him down. "Hey," I said softly, "I'm here." I searched for his soul in those beautiful eyes, and with my own soulful look at him, confirmed for both of us that I wasn't going anywhere. I tried touching and exploring him, hoping he would understand that we had all night under that magical Zimbabwean sky. But soon after, without touching me at all, he was ready again. Thank goodness my body had better sense than I did: My pelvis refused to let him enter, and eventually, after what seemed like hours of him pushing one way and me pushing the other, his semen exploded on my thigh. Afterward, I lay there hugging my knees, listening to him snoring, as tears ran down my face.

That experience made me realize that it was okay to wait to have intercourse, that my creeping age wasn't reason enough to be with someone who wasn't special and willing to take it slow. Since that night, I made a self-promise: I will never put myself in that situation again. And so far, my resolve hasn't been too hard because most of the guys I've met have had predictable reactions once they find out that I'm a virgin. George, David, and Craig, whom I dated on separate occasions, each wanted to put me on a pedestal. I was the "nice girl," the one they wanted to marry. Larry, Mark, and Shawn each hoped to be the first one to get me into bed. It secretly thrilled each of them that their seed would be the first one I might carry. Every date would be a wrestling match as each tried to convince me that I really wanted it—with him—*now*.

I spent hours with brothers and sisters discussing my choice. Unlike some of my friends, my decision wasn't due to religion. One friend thought sex was something you should only share with your husband. "When you try to do pieces of the package, it just doesn't work. You've got to have the whole thing—the spiritual, physical, mental, and emotional," she'd say.

She was right, but I'm still not convinced that sort of union happens only through marriage.

It's not that I feel unattractive, either, even though I do have those days. Nor am I frigid or naive. On the contrary, I am very comfortable with my body and am often the one to initiate physical interaction.

I like to be held and caressed softly. The hairs on my back rise whenever I feel the brush of bristly hairs against my neck. I love to explore—to kiss eyelashes, to rub my smooth face against a rough bearded one. I like the feel of earlobes against my tongue—the cool softness that meshes so easily with a squeeze or a nibble. I like the look of a guy's body, the sweet sloping of the hips to a narrow "v." And the penis is definitely not something I'm afraid of. As a matter of fact, I can spend hours with some- one who is willing to be patient, exploring the dynamics of male genitalia—the function of this piece versus that one. Most guys are rather amazed at my openness—and shocked at my virginity. I've had many make-out sessions where sex was expected because I so enjoyed each moment of the touch.

But I refuse to deal with the selfishness that often accompa- nies youth. Until I know myself and am with someone who knows himself, I will never be able to demand and obtain the satisfaction of my dreams. But the stories traded at lunch or in locker rooms lacked the soul, and most importantly, the simple joy of a touch, which I liked so much.

I still remember how disgusting I felt on that morning after in Zimbabwe, the day I was to leave. I wanted to run the streets of the city and scream. I wanted to scrub my body and wash his pressure from between my legs. I was in a faraway country where women were far from liberated, and I had been afraid to say no—afraid to admit to myself that I still wasn't ready. It was *my* body, but I felt I would be betraying myself, him, and my friends at home if I pushed him away. I had been willing to go through with the act because I had initiated it, not because my body had awakened to the possibility of joining with his. I now thank goodness that I didn't have intercourse on that balmy night.

My high school friends, instead of scrumptious exchanges, offered battlefront war stories of sex that often ended with the guy's conquest and their feeble surrender. The turf for battle was their insecurity, and the scars received were emotional wounds of infidelity. As I listened, I realized that the lack of sharing and joy in these relationships proved that no matter how much my friends were "sexing," many of them were just as virginal as I.

"Girl, we knocked the boots last night!" means nothing if all he did was enter and pump away. And trust me, that's what my friends' boyfriends were doing. My dream lover has to know that sex is more than just a pounding on the pelvis or an act that ends with the release of his semen. He has to have an imagination that matches my own.

I admit I've felt lonely at times. But I'm waiting for someone who will be patient and who will uphold my image of self and sexuality. I dream of gentleness, of walking through the city with my lover and having him point out a single flower that has pushed its way through the cracks of the cement sidewalk. Or my lover and me standing naked in front of the window and imagining ourselves flying past the skyscrapers and smog to the openness above. I want to explore, touch, and discover my body, his body, and all the wonders of lovemaking.

I blame the lack of participation in the act and understanding partly on youth. How can you know the intricate wonders of lovemaking if you're still trying to mentally ground yourself and grow up emotionally?

Lately, though, it seems a powerful energy has begun to translate positively for women when expressed sexually. Women are beginning to stand up and demand satisfaction from sex. The music of my generation echos the sentiments of young women from around the way who are breaking away from the macho images of femininity to author their own roles.

My girlfriends are now talking about orgasms and masturbation. Women are discovering their own bodies and letting brothers know it's not just about them getting theirs. They're *touching* themselves and demanding that guys *touch* them, too.

I know a lot more about myself now. And because of my decision, sex translates to *empowerment*. I'm finally in a caring relationship where tenderness is the norm. I'm looking forward to further exploring the sexual part of myself. I look forward to the day when my boyfriend—who is unafraid of being free, who wants to share and enjoy life and revel in the simplicity of touching, and whose view of female sexuality is not limited to his own pleasure—takes my hand, and we escape to the limitless boundaries of our imaginations.

Unlike *Webster's Ninth Collegiate Dictionary*, which says a virgin is "free of impurity or stain; chaste; modest; unsullied," I've come to believe that a virgin is a woman who is whole within herself, someone who doesn't feel she must belong to a man.

In the beginning of time, virginity had more to do with sexual independence than with sexual chastity . The word virgin was derived from a Latin root, Virgo, meaning strength, force, skill. I like that. My ideal woman is a woman with her tightly coiled 'fro, and taut—but not waifish—body in the tropical isles, giving and receiving physical pleasure, and in charge of her own soul.

Even if it means I'm the last one left, I hope to remain a virgin all my life.

House Arrest

by Tayari Jones

Dear Diary,

I hate men. There is nothing to eat in this house and it is all because of them. I got home from work a little late today. By the time I had gotten in, the sun had already set. It's cold enough in the daytime, but at night it's even worse—I feel like the winter wind is going to rip my clothes right off.

I put on my coat and got as far as the door. By the time I would have made it to the store, it would have been night. I put my coat back on the hanger. I guess I'll try to go tomorrow.

Dear Diary,

I got home late again today. This is getting ridiculous. Here I am, still afraid of the dark.

I ordered a pizza, but when the delivery man rang the bell, I was afraid to open the door.

"Who is it?" I said.

"Pizza," he said back.

I looked out of the peephole. There was a man standing there in a red shirt, red cap, and holding a red container that was about the size of a pizza. I put my hand on the knob, but I couldn't make myself twist my wrist.

I hate men.

Dear Diary,

Got home late again. But I refused to go another day without decent food. I decided to go to the store. I laced up my boots, wrapped my wool scarf tight around me, grabbed my mace, put my list in my coat pocket, and headed out the door. The store is only two blocks away. If it weren't for the trees, I could see it from my doorstep.

Halfway there, I heard the sound of rubber shoe soles hitting asphalt. I knew that I should either speed up or slow down. I decided to walk really slow so that whoever it was could pass me and I could keep an eye on him. He was a guy, about eighteen, I guess. Anyway, he walked by. As he was passing me, he turned and looked my way.

He didn't say anything or do anything scary; he just looked.

I felt so stupid. My heart fell down through my boots. I slowed some, to put space between us. Finally he turned the corner. I just turned around and ran all of the way home. This is getting out of hand. I have been living on peanut butter and dry cornflakes for three days.

Dear Diary,

TGIF!! I *finally* got my groceries. I had a date with Terrence. On the way back from the movies, I asked him if we could stop off at the store. You should have seen the look on his face as I started filling up a buggy. He must have thought that I just needed to pick up a couple of things. But a person's gotta do what she's gotta do.

Now I have enough groceries to last me for the rest of my life—almost. I even bought dried milk and eggs like they tell you to when there is a storm coming.

Dear Diary,

It has been a long time since I have been out with a guy that I was not prepared to kill. Sometimes it makes me feel guilty. Terrence is a really nice person. My mother would *love* him. I feel like such an impostor sitting next to him at the movies pretending to laugh, knowing good and well that I have practiced killing him at least a thousand times.

Dear Diary,

It's been a year ago today.

Dear Diary,

Mom wants me to see a counselor. I think "paranoid" was the word she used. She saw a tabloid talk show or something and now she is convinced that I am suffering from Post Traumatic Stress Disorder. Jeez. What do I look like, a Vietnam vet?

Anyway, if a counselor is going to play games with my mind and convince me that the world is made of sunshine, I don't want to go. Been there. Done that. A person has got to be careful these days. Rosy glasses may be in style, but studies have shown that they can be hazardous to your health.

Oh, that reminds me. Did you know that almost any household item can be used as a weapon? I read that somewhere.

Dear Diary,

I smashed my TV today. If my mother had seen me do it, she'd put me in the crazy house in a New York minute. But I am not crazy. Not at all. I was watching this murder mystery about this guy who was chopping women's fingers off and putting them in sandwich bags. That's when I smashed my TV. You would have done the same thing if you could have seen it.

I wanted to take it out to the dump, but it was really dark outside. I drank a vodka tonic and tried to go to sleep. Took a Valium. That helped.

Dear Diary,

Michael asked me out. I think I hurt his feelings when I said no. I wasn't trying to be mean, but I didn't want to give him the wrong idea. It is so easy to send out the wrong messages from the way you bat your eyelashes or cross your legs. It is not his fault. And anyway, he is just so big. His fist is as big as my face.

Dear Diary,

It has been a year and a week. You can never forget, can you?

Dear Diary,

I know Mama thinks that I have lost it. I never should have told her about it in the first place. I wish she would stop pestering me. I wouldn't be surprised if I found out that she carries a collapsible counselor in her purse.

I could use another drink.

Dear Diary,

Mama keeps bringing it up. She keeps complaining that I am cutting her off. What more is there to say? I gave her all the details a year ago. Is she trying to rub it in? I was stupid. I made a mistake. I admit it. I should have known better than to walk home alone after dark. I've learned from it. I am a lot more careful now. How am I supposed to live my life if she keeps bringing it up all of the time?

Dear Diary,

I wonder if "drinking yourself to death" is just a figure of speech. If not, I wonder how long it would take. It must be an expression, or else I would have *been* dead.

Dear Diary,

If I had thought of it earlier, I would have mother-proofed my bathroom. She's disturbed my sleeping pills. She's disturbed my bath brush ("You actually use that on your *skin*?"). She's even taken to counting the number of showers I take per day. This is getting ridiculous.

Dear Diary,

He said he would kill me if I screamed. Knowing what I know now, and assuming he is a man of his word, I should have hollered loud enough to shame the devil.

Dear Diary,

I saw him today. In the grocery store. He was buying eggs and milk, just like me. He looked right through me like he had never seen me. I tried to get out before he recognized me, but it was so confusing with the little signs saying THIS AISLE CLOSED and the electric doors with the arrows and the words saying USE OTHER DOOR. Before I could get out, I was so scared that I vomited. Right there in Food Mart. Three feet from the exit. Then it went dark. Somebody called an ambulance.

Mom stayed all night with me in the hospital, but all she did was cry. I didn't say anything.

The world is wrong and I am tired of being in it.

Dear Diary,

I have been in bed a week now. Mama keeps intercepting my calls. It's okay. I don't feel like talking to anyone anyway. I think that Mama is happy about the Grocery Store Incident. I don't think she is glad that I saw him, or that I was alone, or that I threw up. But I think that she is glad that she has the chance to baby me. I think she feels bad because she was not there when the first incident (we have to number them) happened. But it is not her fault. After all, a person expects her grown child to be able to take care of herself.

Dear Diary,

I think that the fun of playing nurse has worn off for Mama, because now she cries all the time. When she comes into my room, she is smiling in a stiff way like someone said "say cheese" and she is waiting for the flash. Then I hear her crying in the bathroom. The echo carries.

"Just stand on the balcony," she said. "Some fresh air will do you good."

I looked out of the glass door and saw a tree with spindly things hanging off of the branches like little Christmas ornaments. I wanted to go outside and pull one down. But I couldn't.

Mama cried some more. I wish I could just stand out there like everyone else, making careless chitchat about how spring is almost here now. Maybe then Mama would sleep a little. Eat a little.

Dear Diary,

I sat in bed this morning with fourteen Valium cupped in my left hand and a glass of vodka on my nightstand. I had to decide. I couldn't go on being too scared to live and petrified of dying. I don't know how long I sat vacillating, weighing out the pros and the cons. I undid the lock and opened up the window. There was nothing much going on outside. Just people walking to the Laundromat with their baskets, folks getting into and out of their cars, little kids running to catch a yellow bus. Just a typical morning. By the time I finished watching and thinking, the capsules had gotten mushy from the heat in my hand.

I went and checked the mailbox. My legs were like overcooked spaghetti. I could hear my blood crashing against my temples. My head hurt so bad that I had to close my eyes and rest halfway down the walkway. I held my right hand steady with my left in order to do the combination on the mailbox. The sixth time was the charm.

When I got back in the house and handed Mama the junk mail, she gave me a look that I couldn't quite place at first. It was as if we'd really won the million dollars promised to us by the Publisher's Clearing House sweepstakes. Mama was proud of me. I guess I didn't recognize the expression on her face at first because I hadn't seen it in so long.

Dear Diary,

I can't believe how warm it was today. Spring isn't officially here yet. One more week to go. . . .

I went to get the paper today. By myself. Mama wasn't at the door looking out to make sure I made it safe. She slept late this morning. (Can you believe it?) So, I got the paper and opened it up. Although I never thought that I was the center of the universe, I was surprised at how much went on without me.

When Mama woke up, I was just lying on the floor with the paper stretched out around me. She looked at me and shook her head, but not in that nervous way that means she is trying not to cry. She just shook her head in a motherly kind of way, stepped over me, and went into the kitchen to fix herself some coffee.

There were six births announced in the newspaper yesterday. Can you believe that? And think of all those women who just had their babies, took them home, and didn't bother to tell the papers. So many new people. I wonder how many were born while I was trapped in this apartment? Thirty? A hundred maybe? And that is just in this city. Can you imagine how many were born in the world?

Dear Diary,

Going to get the paper has become my little routine. It's really not that hard. Kind of fun, actually. When I read the paper, I always turn right to the birth announcements.

Dear Diary,

You will not believe how much weight I have lost. I tried on my blue suit and it was hanging off me. Thank God for alterations.

Today I looked at the want ads. I know the economy is bad, but it seems that a lot of people are wanted to do a bunch of different things. There are a lot of listings that I know nothing about, but a few of them look pretty interesting. I put circles around them with a fat green marker. I wonder how long it will take the tailor to take in my skirt? Do you think that my old job will give me a decent reference? Ha! I can just see it. "She was really good at her job, until she lost her mind."

Dear Diary,

Old people say that what doesn't kill you makes you stronger. Now, I can't say that I believe that. There are a lot of things that can happen to you that can shake your confidence and turn you from a regular person into a shivering wreck. (I should know, I spent six months not being able to tell my ass from my elbow.) But I think that what doesn't kill me, doesn't kill me, and there is no use pretending to be dead if I'm not.

Dear Diary,

I went out in my blue suit that looks like a completely different suit since I had it altered. But I think that it looked pretty good on me anyway. I had an interview. I rode the subway—all by myself, just me and my mace (always have to have my mace).

On the train, I sat next to a woman who was holding this fat little baby on her lap. I know that this is the city and you're not supposed to look at people, but this baby was so cute that nobody could stop looking at her and making faces and stupid little noises. She just gurgled and laughed for the next three stops. Then she looked over at me and held her little arms out. I didn't know what to do—this is the city and you just can't be taking people's children off their laps. But the woman said, "Go ahead and hold her." I could tell that she was from Africa because she had some kind of accent.

I put the baby on my lap and I could smell that sweet baby, who smelled like lotion, powder, and milk. When I got to my stop, I gave the child back to her mother. I took so long thanking her that I missed my stop and had to get off at the next one and walk back. It didn't bother me much, because it was a very pretty day. The kind poets live for.

The interview was in this big glass building downtown. In front of it was a huge flower bed. From a distance, the different colors spelled out the name of the company, but from where I was, they just looked like so many flowers growing together. Like God was working overtime. On my way home, I pulled up one of the flowers—the whole thing, roots and all. Then I threw the coffee out of my cup and put the flower and some dirt in it. I decided to walk all the way home because I didn't want the cup to be knocked out of my hand on the busy subway.

I planted it in a flower box right outside my window. That way I can watch it grow.

Dear Diary,

Green thumbs say that transplants almost never work. Maybe they don't, but my flower is thriving out there. You should see it! The bloom is almost open all of the way and those fat bumblebees can't stay away from it!

Mama said that it looked like a tiny explosion of color. She's right.

A Bond of Love
by Corliss Hill

In my family, special friendships between mothers and daughters have been passed down through generations like the colorful quilts my foremothers made by hand. So when my grandmother passed away, I tried hard to understand my mother's emptiness and sorrow. At age eleven, I worked desperately to fill the void in my mother's life by either cleaning the house, doing well in school, or simply making her laugh. My mother also tried to remain strong, but I remember holding her and dabbing her teary eyes when the pain hit too hard. My own tears fell in darkness but I dared not let her see that I, too, longed to see my grandmother again.

I believe that period was a turning point for me and my mom. Sure, my father was supportive along with other family and friends, but our bond is what made the difference. My mom had always been in my corner and this was a time for me to help her make it through one of the most difficult times of her life. We had reached the first level of a maturing friendship.

As my best friend, I shared practically everything with her, which surprised some of my girlfriends. We even hung out—scouring malls, shopping centers, and garage sales for the best bargains. Yeah, Mom and I had a cool relationship, but it was still difficult for me to share an intimate part of me—my sexuality. But I never thought sex would be the issue that put my friendship with my mom to the test. Her interrogations about my virginity during high school were as commonplace as getting zits. Though I always managed to change the subject or dodge the answer, I had become tired of lying to my mother. If I was mature enough to engage in sex, then I was mature enough to finally confide in my mother, right? Wrong. Unfortunately, I realized that after the fact. Owning up to my mother about having sex at age eighteen wasn't exactly the ideal situation.

My mother—a prim and proper traditional woman from a small town in Georgia—couldn't bear the idea of her only teenage daughter having premarital sex. Having grown up in a household of sweet but stern black women with down-home morals and a Georgia Peach value system, the topic of sex was never discussed. But my mom *did* break the traditional barriers of silence by lecturing me every time I went out with my boyfriend.

"Keep your legs closed and your panties on," sprang from her mouth at least once a week. "You have too much going for you. These little boys want only one thing anyway. Plus, I'm not ready to be a grandmother."

The lectures were so constant that I learned to tune them out. When Mom entered into this mode, I viewed her as "my mother," rather than the woman I had learned to cultivate such a close relationship with. It was in these moments that I realized what I was up against—a friendship that couldn't withstand the blow of my growing sexuality.

The day I finally told my mother the truth is one that I'll never forget. I had just arrived home at three-thirty in the morning after having *forbidden* sex with my boyfriend. Already in a bad mood, my mother met me at the top of the stairs with tousled hair and a "You better have a good excuse" expression plastered on her face. I was late coming home and my mom demanded an answer without even saying a word. Her twisted lips and squinted eyes were clear signs of disgust. She interrupted my explanation with only one question: "Have you been having sex?"

The words felt like someone had just knocked me right off my feet. Walking into my bedroom, with Mom right on my heels, I somehow gathered the strength to finally come clean. But I never expected her reaction. She banged her fists on the edge of my bed pleading and whispering, "Lord, have mercy. Lord, please have mercy on me today!"

As I look back on that predawn morning, I'll never forget the piercing look of disappointment on my mother's face after I admitted to her I was sexually active. Now that some time has passed, I have a better understanding of my mother's feelings. The only thing that still puzzles me is why, at three-thirty in the morning, she felt compelled to get out of bed, get fully dressed, grab her coat, and go for a drive. Well, I suppose this was part of her coping process.

Prior to that morning, I never thought about approaching my mother with the topic of sex. After all, I was "too young and immature to handle this act and its many consequences." Also, I was worried about jeopardizing our great relationship or tainting the image of the "respectable young lady" she raised me to be.

But on the other hand, I wanted so desperately to express my newfound womanhood to my mother. It seemed as though all of my other girlfriends' mothers knew of their sexual curiosity or activity. Their mothers were even making appointments for them at the gynecologist's office or pushing the idea of birth control pills on them. The only thing my mother was pushing on me were college and scholarship applications.

Actually, I think my mother was in denial about me blossoming into a young woman. Her little girl was fading fast, and a woman was taking form. I needed to make my own decisions without her approval. She had done a wonderful job of instilling values in me about life's lessons, and it was now time for me to use these tools for life's tests. I was a young woman who wanted to venture out and learn from my mistakes. My mother just didn't want me to make any mistakes that would hurt me for a lifetime.

On that tension-filled morning, the last thing I heard my mother say when she returned from her thirty-minute drive was: "We'll talk later in the morning." I reluctantly agreed.

To my surprise, Mom had prepared a list of questions, and expected answers to each and every one. I, on the other hand, didn't plan to answer any I felt invaded my privacy.

At the onset of the conversation, I remember stating my personal reasons for becoming sexually active. I had fallen in love for the first time and thought the only way to express love in its highest form was by having sex. My boyfriend and I were mature enough to know what we were doing and had also given it careful contemplation. Sure, some of my other friends were sexually active but their actions had no effect upon my decision. I even told my mother that I was willing to take full responsibility for any consequences. I was confident, actually a bit cocky, because I just *knew* that I had all the bases covered.

What I hadn't prepared for was Mom's interrogation: "What are you going to do if you get pregnant?"; "Is the relationship exclusive, and how do you really know if it is or not?" ; "Where in the hell have you been having sex? Not in my house, I hope!"; "What type of protection have the two of you been using?"; "How many times have you had sex?" ; "Do you know that you may be putting your life in jeopardy?"; "What made you want to have sex? Peer pressure?"

There was no way that I would or even *could* answer all of those questions. The confident young woman in me had shrunk back down to a little girl who carelessly disobeyed her mother. For about two hours, we talked, yelled, listened, and even cried together. We had finally reached a realm of the mother-daughter relationship where friendship is put to the test.

We both made an effort to remain calm throughout the conversation but my mother forgot that she raised me to be just as strong-willed as she, so neither one of us backed down from our respective viewpoints. She felt betrayed by my dishonesty. And I felt trapped by her standards. I couldn't understand how she encouraged me to talk to her about everything except sex. On the other hand, my mother was disappointed and didn't understand why sex was such a concern of mine. Bottom line: We were two different people, with two different perspectives, who grew up in very different times. Coming from worlds apart, we'd have to work hard to find a happy medium.

Today, the subject of sex doesn't come up often between us. But when it does, the tension that once existed is no longer there. I attribute this to the fact that neither one of us abandoned our beliefs and opinions but learned to respect each other's judgment. We got through this sensitive period because of our strong bond of love and friendship. Ironically, that trying experience helped open more doors of communication.

But there was still one missing piece to the puzzle. What was the purpose of that early-morning drive? When I asked my mother about it, she said, "Live long enough, have children and then, you'll understand."

When the day arises, I wonder how I'll react when I find out that my daughter is no longer that "sweet, innocent" virgin. Will I, too, go for a drive, and if I do, where will I go?

I guess I can always call my best friend, Mom, and ask her for directions.

MammaSea and Me
by Anasuya Isaacs

I am six and a half and you can't tell me nothing. Three years of reading has made me an expert and I let everyone know it. I have potty trained my baby brother who just turned five, and I'm working on his reading. He's a bit slow but I know he'll get it. I have two best friends: my left thumb, which is a warm blanket, a sweet lollipop, and a hug all rolled into one; and Tabu, my chocolate-drop doll with the super Afro. The three of us go everywhere together.

I am six and a half and we're playing in my godmother's backyard, where Ma can see us through the sliding glass doors. My brother suggests that we go over to that field next to the parking lot behind her yard.

With our homemade swords, we fight and run and fall and kill each other at least a dozen times. Then we decide to play tag-and-seek: a mixture of hide-and-seek and tag. It's my turn to find my brother. I look everywhere for him till I nearly give up. I warn him that I'm gonna beat him up for cheating.

All of a sudden, he grabs me from behind. I say, "Boy, I'm chasing *you*," as I turn around. I gasp when I see a strange-looking man dressed all in white. He's shaking me and holding me tighter as I try to pull away. I scream to my brother to help me. The man covers my mouth. I keep trying to scream, even though it's hard to breathe. He's covering my nose, too. I'm crying. Why is he holding me?

My brother comes running with a brick. He hits the boogey-man against the leg. The boogeyman gets mad. He lets go of my mouth so that one of his hands is free. I scream "run!" but my brother doesn't move. He starts to throw rocks and sticks and whatever else is handy until the boogeyman whacks him across the head with the brick. I scream as I watch my brother go down, blood pouring out of his head.

I break away and run toward the apartment but the boogeyman catches me by the foot and drags me on my back toward him. As he rips my shorts and my monogrammed panties off, I pass out.

I come to in a big bright white room. People are talking in hushed tones about rape and a little girl. I feel a sucking of air scrape between my legs. Watching my brother fall to the ground, blood flowing from his head flashes in my head. I scream. Then I immediately reach for my thumb, best friend #1, and for the first time, I become aware that it is throbbing. I start to cry because the rest of me is throbbing, too. I pull my left thumb to comfort me and discover to my horror that it is all bandaged up. The shock causes me to pass out again.

I am six and a half, and on the witness stand. The courtroom is dark. The only light I see is coming from the windows where I fix my stare. The judge tells me I don't have to say anything if I don't want to. Just nod my head yes or no when they ask me a question.

The man in the suit asks me if the man who attacked me and my brother is in the room. Without turning from the window, I nod yes. Then he asks me to point to that man so that everyone will know who he is. I quickly turn my head toward him, point and turn back to the window. The nice judge tells me I don't have to do anything else so I can step down. I walk real fast past the table where the boogeyman is sitting. When I get to my chair, I see that my mother is crying. I take her hand and tell her it's not her fault. Then they call my brother to the witness stand. I tell him it's okay when I see that he wants to cry, too. I tell myself that if I have to cry, I'll cry later. I can say that because I know that when I get home I'll go hide underneath my covers and disappear into the underwater world of MammaSea that is waiting for me.

I dive like a dolphin
into the crystal blue silence
offered me by MammaSea
whose children sing to me of a treasure,
found in the valley of their mother's bosom.
They call me to them: "Come see and be part of we
come see and be part of we."
I dive in and now I am one of MammaSea's children.

I must learn how to sing
and this frightens me so.
I'm afraid I'll drown, and on my face it shows.
Mamma's seaweed fingers hush me.
In my ear she whispers, "Be like the starfish
and cling to the darkened depths of my safe salty soul."

My fear begins to float away.
MammaSea already knows that I long forgot
how a sun-kiss feels on the back of my neck;
how I used to trade secrets with the wind;
how a moonray once asked me to dance with her real slow
under its light.

MammaSea already knows
that the world of land offers me no melody,

no clan, no treasure,
no bosom in which to crawl and forget my pain.

MammaSea knows all about me.
She wants me for her own.

I am nine going on ten, but in the eyes of the men I pass on the street as I go to get candy from Miss Friedman's store, I am not a child. Those men speak to me ever so courteously but with eyes full of lust. I am nine going on ten, but to my uncle who has taken me to be his special playmate since we came to live with Grandma while Ma goes back to school, I am more than a kid.

"No, your brother can't play with us," my uncle says. "Only special little girls," he explains to me each time I beg him to let my brother come along. He tells me it's our secret and that no one should know. "Not even Ma?" I ask. "Especially not her. She'll send you away to be adopted and you'll never see her again."

I am nine going on ten, but since my innocence was stripped away, ripped away from me like my favorite panties that had the day monogrammed on them (was it Saturday or Sunday that I lost forever?), I've become less of a child.

I am nine going on ten, or is it nine going on twenty? I have already rationalized why I have to take the quarters my uncle gives me to slide his thing between my ballerina thighs. He's quick. I just stare at the radiator until I become hard and cold and gray, just like the radiator itself. But I just hate it when that warm wet stuff squirts all over my T-shirt, or worse, on my leg.

I am nine going on ten, but I'm not dumb. I know good and well that letting him lock the door behind me is a small price to pay to keep my mother from killing him; to keep her from going to jail; to keep my brother and me from being orphaned since Daddy is already dead and gone; to keep anyone from knowing that I am getting paid to do it just like the girls on the street corners.

I am nine going on ten, and I begin my descent, slowly but most definitely into the not-here world where little girls can escape big men. I slide like a penguin into my crystal-blue silence. MammaSea doesn't make us talk if we don't want to. But she encourages us to sing, which is fine by me. I couldn't find the spoken words anyway. I just don't have words to convey that my thighs are raw and that it does not feel good when my stiff body is pried wide open. I just don't have words to convey my terror when I nearly suffocate under the expanse of my uncle's large frame. I just don't have words to say that it hurts, that tears are rolling down my face, that I don't like playing this game. So, I escape,

> *I stand at the edge of the ocean.*
> *The roar of the crashing waves*
> *hypnotically invite me to swim with the dolphins and with*
> *MammaSea.*
>
> *I allow the waves to swallow me whole*
> *To pull me deep into MammaSea's bosom*
> *To take me away*
> *so that no one can ask me what's wrong*
> *so that I can't see that no one asks me what's wrong*
> *so that I can't hear that no one asks me what's wrong*
> *so that I can act like nothing is wrong*
> *. . . for now*

I am almost thirteen and oh God, my head is throbbing. I wish it would fall off. The pain only intensifies when I see that my face resembles a blue-black gourd. I must really be despicable if I can get my mother to hate me enough to do this to me. I bring her shame.

I don't fit in anywhere, though I try so hard. I'll never be like the other kids, nice and ordinary. Though my mother always says "dare to be different," she always asks me why I can't be normal. I haven't a clue as to what normal is but I'm convinced it's my fault that I'm not. If I were normal, then I would be good enough. My mother wouldn't be ashamed of me. She would love me. If I were normal, she wouldn't try to kill me with her wooden clog. She would hug me, and tell me how pretty I am, tell me how smart I am, tell me she wouldn't trade me in for the world.

But I'm laying on the cold bathroom floor, sobbing painfully as I realize that I'll never be good enough because I was ruined, soiled, damaged, a long time ago. And though I never told her about my uncle, my scarlet "D" for Damaged must be visible to her. Mothers know everything. I don't blame mine for hating me. Sometimes I think I made those guys do that to me. Maybe she thinks the same thing, too.

I am almost thirteen and I am painfully aware of the futility of my life. I ask myself what's the point? I'm not bringing any happiness to the world. To the contrary, I seem to bring out the worst in people.

I haven't been able to hide out with MammaSea for a long time. I can't seem to remember how to slip out of my skin and slide into the world of dolphins and starfish. I can't seem to break away anymore, like I used to. I'm forced to stay where I'm not wanted. I'm a burden to my mother who hates me. I don't belong here . . . or anywhere. So I rummage through the medicine cabinet in search of skull and bones.

Skull and bones, skull and bones. I drink the bitter juice as I try to forget the feel of Ma's clog against my head. I drink to forget the feel of that same clog against my chest. I drink to forget the wild rage, the screams, the chase, the slipping in and out of consciousness. I drink to make sure this is the last time I hear her say she is sick of me. I drink the bitter juice of skull and bones so that I can stop breathing; so I can stop the need to escape to the sea from the empty shell that I call me; so I can stop the throbbing in my body, the only proof that there is something still alive in here, somewhere.

I am almost thirteen as I wait for my arteries to be filled with this strange juice. I debate whether to write a good-bye letter or not. What would I say? What could ink on paper say that seven years of blood flowing from my eyes could not do? No. No good-bye letter. I'll leave those around me wrapped in the comfort of their ignorance. "Forgive them, Father, for they know not what they did or didn't do," I pray as I slip into the heaven-bound chariot, smiling.

The cold porcelain floor greets me as I violently hurl my insides into the darkness. My body trembles. I am not sure where I am. My heart is racing. Am I leaving my human body so that I can enter into the next realm, into heaven?

When all that is left to hurl is my very skin and bones, and my trembling subsides for a moment, I figure out that I am truly in my bathroom. On earth. I lay there staring at the ceiling, in shock. Why am I still alive? Why have I been sent back here to suffer? Even God doesn't love me enough to take me away from here? Warm tears roll down, stinging me as they slide over my welts and open scars, and moisten the collar of my pajamas. As the tears roll, I hear a voice that says God has saved me for a reason. The voice coming from inside the cave of my being is sweet, like MammaSea's songs. A warm glow fills me in a way I've never felt before. And it's responding directly to my questions by glowing brighter and hotter. I finally have what I've been looking for all my life: confirmation that somebody, some Power, cares about me. Somebody *does* love me. Now I know from the depths of my being that my life from this moment on will never be the same.

As time passes, I am guided by the sweet voice that has been everything to me: sister-friend, confidante, guardian angel, warm blanket. Slowly my fear of the past duplicating itself in my future is eroding as I become secure in my understanding of who I really am: a strong woman; and who I am becoming: a child who is free to love everybody (even men) unconditionally.

I do all I can to protect the me-to-be with songs of praise for my beauty, my purity, and my joy. For the first time in my life I feel like I can stop running, stop hiding, stop pretending I'm someone else, something else, anything else, except me.

For the first time in a long time, I call out to the six-year-old me who lost her voice with her monogrammed panties to come out of the sea, to come out of hiding. To come out and let me take care of her, to protect her.

Slowly, I start to take my place in this crazy, wonderful world. With open arms I welcome myself and hug the pain away; hug the scars away; hug the silence away. And for the first time ever, I thank God for saving me from that cold bathroom floor.

In time, I have become lighter and more joyful. The burden of carrying my cross alone for all of these years is slowly lifting as I start to share what I've overcome with those who are close to me. In doing so, I realize that silence has been both my greatest comfort and my greatest prison. So I'm beginning to trust again. For the first time since my last game of tag, I feel protected and safe. Safe enough to allow myself to actually *feel* again.

MammaSea would be proud of me. Once again, I know how a sun-kiss feels on the nape of my neck and how to kiss back without getting burned. I can now trade secrets with the wind, and in exchange she's teaching me how to fly!

The Menstrual Hut

by Eisa Nefertari Ulen

Guys have always moved in and out of my life, and I expect this will continue until I'm married and a mother. But the circles of women in my life have remained constant. Their influences on me are ever-present. And when I really stop to think about it, it seems that generations of women have always thrived together—away from men.

The menstrual hut, where women of ancient African cultures often lived during the nights and days of their menstrual cycles, has always appealed to me. It used to be that girls were banished from their villages, ostracized because of blood loss—sent to the menstrual hut. I can't help envisioning these huts as powerhouses where women would bleed together regularly and share the deepest parts of themselves. Today, we form our "menstrual huts" during our hair-braiding sessions on the front stoop, and at Girl Scout meetings, and when we're just plain laughing with each other.

Before my first menstrual cycle, I was a girl who ran free and wild near the hills of Appalachia—short 'fro, cut-off shorts, tube top, and me. Each day the creeks and trees called me to play. And I did. I climbed tall branches to offer Wind a better ear. I swam across waters that wound toward the sea. I lay in green fields as Earth tossed and turned beneath my back. And, when I felt the unspoken call of my mother to return home, I raced, covered with

Pennsylvania soil, to our doorstep. Mommy told me to strip and run straight to the shower (she didn't want me tracking dirt in her house). Mommy and I lived alone and existed together comfortably in one large room.

Our bodies grew together—mine moved into puberty and my mother's further into womanhood. The sight of her mature body helped me respect my own body, which was coming into womanhood. Her body belonged to me; or rather, I saw my future self in her grown-up contours.

The part of Mommy that truly amazed me was that dark triangle of hair out of which I knew blood sometimes flowed—and out of which I, too, had flowed not many years ago. That, to me, was power. Lush, like the tops of the trees I climbed; liquid strength, like the waters where I swam; black like the earth that cradled trees and creeks and me. One day I would know the power of that special female place within me—because a circle of women offered me a strong girlhood.

When I was a young child, this tiny, spirited community of women surrounded me: Mommy and me strong and together in the center; Grandmom and my aunt; their women friends; and older cousins I called aunties surrounding us.

When I was a little girl, I loved to sit cross-legged, my hair braided, holding one of Grandmom's homemade frozen strawberry daiquiris. Mommy, Grandmommy, and I would sit and talk all night, laughing and sipping the sweet cold of freshly squeezed berries out of old glasses. From those talks, which were rich with the stories of mothers and aunts and friends of aunts, I learned lessons of loving. When we talked about sex, I learned how wonderful it would feel. Mommy and Grandmom also taught me that the pain for loving could sometimes hurt. My aunties helped me understand what it would feel like to let someone into your body.

They told me I needed to think about my body, then sex would bring the greatest pleasure. They taught me selection.

As I moved from girlhood to womanhood, I giggled at slumber parties about tampons and "doing it." My friends and I talked about becoming women. We read *Are You There, God? It's Me, Margaret* by Judy Blume. On weekends my friends would come to visit with *their* mothers and my circle of women grew wider and stronger around me.

By the time my body went through its first menstrual cycle, I had danced without Mommy at basement parties. I was learning that my body fit nicely against a boy's body. I was beginning to enjoy the feel of hands that weren't my own on my hips. I was beginning to like the way the heat at those parties made my sweaty hair puff out, and my shirt stick to me so that it showed off the lines of my training bra.

Soon I was tongue kissing Lil' Marky, a boy who had a gold tooth. He was so much shorter than I was that we had to sit on the back steps of my apartment building so his lips could reach mine.

I learned that boys were fun—enjoyable in more ways than I'd known before. I could still beat most of them in swimming races. But when some of them wanted to play other games, like touching the names on my designer jeans, I started to understand that hanging out with boys wasn't as simple as it was before.

In high school I opened the rim of my female friendship circle even wider and added my own friends to the mix. My two closest sister-friends and I loved to talk about sex (we no longer referred to it as "doing it") and we frequently weighed the big question: should I make my high school sweetheart "the first"? One thought I should; the other thought I shouldn't, but the influences of those from my inner circle remained strongest. Mommy and Grandmom counseled me to wait until I was just a little bit older, and I did.

My first real boyfriend knew my body better than any guy before him. We had spent so many months getting to know each other. When we first made love, it was perfect. I had attended a banquet that night, so I wore a black taffeta dress. My lipstick shined and my skin glowed from the kisses of summer sun. I can still feel that first feeling. It still feels wonderful. My body connected to his and we moved in such a perfect rhythm. From the beginning I loved sex. And I knew Mommy and Grandmom would be happy for me.

So after about a week or two I sat with one knee crossed over the other and told my mother about it. She smiled for me, but I could feel something quiet and sad give a little in her. The next time I saw Grandmom, I told her, too, and tears filled her eyes. I asked her why she was crying—she always said she would feel happy for me when I finally fell in love and chose to share my love. She told me she did feel happy, but she also felt a little sad for herself. When I told her I would always be her little girl, she smiled and nodded, but explained that I would belong to her differently now.

I still don't know what this means. Perhaps when my daughter speaks to me about giving love, I'll understand what mothers must feel as they watch their girls grow. Maybe I'll also smile—happy for their exploration, but sad for myself.

After my first time, I enjoyed two great long-term relationships. Then I met someone who cared *about* me, but not enough *for* me. Strong, fine, talented, he slipped in and then, just like that, he left.

To struggle through my sadness, I found myself reaching back for the women who had offered me guidance along the way. To understand where I needed to go, I called on Mommy, Grandmom, my aunties, and my sister-friends. I remember not being able to wait to get home, to sit in the kitchen and listen. I knew that while I smelled their delicious cooking, I would hear the voices of strong black women who loved and nurtured me since my conception. I knew, too, that men would stay out of our way. We would talk, and I would learn more women secrets.

Sure enough, after spending time with the women who have always given me so much, I got the strength and solace I needed. From my circle of support I learned that love like my first time returns again. Sometimes again and again. Mostly I learned that men may slip away, but that women are always there for me.

My greatest strength, I now know, has always contained the spiraling circles of women—with their seriousness, giggles, whispers, shouts, and tears. Like chants and spells, our talk creates healing and understanding. Through centuries we women have bled together, and discovered our similarities.

This simple truth has remained strong for me. For it is because of the open sharing I've enjoyed with other women that I felt a cyst on my mother's ovary and learned what to feel for on myself. This is why, as I was dressing with Grandmommy, I discovered that she, too, had a heavy menstrual flow when she was a young woman.

In our women's temple I witness the changes of life and what they mean to me. Although many of the women in my circle are older and at different life stages, I am learning that these older women radiate new spirit and energy. I can dance and feel good about myself because my circle of women has taught me to shake my body and love it.

These wise women have taught me the signs of danger—a man who might hit you, who might cheat you—and the signs of wonder—a man who will caress you, and who will help you grow.

Through the support of women, I've come to learn that the strength of my love flows from an understanding of myself. Sometimes I reach up in the soft darkness of my room and feel the air above my bed. I feel my body stretch. And then, just when I'm lost in the feeling of the air above me, I pull my arms back to myself. There, I feel what my mother has touched in her bed at night and my grandmother has, too—self. And knowing that I am here to love myself in the night, in the day, in my life, feels good.

I have learned to listen to my body as Mommy listens to hers. I have learned to talk to women friends about our bodies as my mother has spoken to her friends.

These are gifts that I can only find in the menstrual hut. They're gifts that keep me fully alive.

My Trip Down Celebrity Lane
by Lisa Chestnut-Chapman

Dear Cuz:

I know I haven't written to you for a while, but so much has been happening, and I am just at a point where I can share it with you. We don't normally talk about sex; your virginal ears and disgusted expressions usually stop the conversation before it goes too far. And because you're my baby cousin (I know only by a year, but what a difference a year makes!), I always feel like I should be protecting you. But speaking out may be good for both of us. And plus, I want you to know what's been going on in my life.

So, okay, here it goes: Somehow an incredible, Grammy-award winning musician entered my world, stopped it in its tracks, and turned it spinning in another direction.

Lord have mercy, that man sent chills down my spine. You see, he plays the sexiest brass instrument in the world and is so supersexy every time he puts its mouthpiece between his lips. Most women can't help but fall in love with this brother. You would, too, especially if you inherited my taste. (When I see you face-to-face, I'll tell you who the guy is, and what instrument he plays. You know how I feel about writing stuff down on paper that I don't want anyone else to see or know about. Remember when my diary was stolen?)

Anyway, when Mr. Celebrity (or Mr. C for short) is not on a stage creating a wildly frantic or smoothly sensual sound that penetrates the soul, he's somewhere in the media causing all kinds of havoc with his sarcastic remarks and overstated opinions. In my book, even after all I'm about to tell you, he is just awesome.

This is how it all started:

A group of celebrities performed at my school's music festival. I wasn't familiar with Mr. C or the group at that time, and hung out in the student center, studying for an exam, while they set up for the concert that was to happen that night.

As luck would have it, Mr. C caught a glimpse of me studying and on the day after the concert sent a classmate to say he wanted to meet me. At first I saw this guy as just another brother, not even my flavor. I can't believe how flip I was about meeting him. "*He* can find *me*," I said with a shake of my hair, like *I* was the star. Please! I was plain stupid or just too naive to see that he was someone to get weak in the knees over. But after a lot of persistence on the part of his friend, I decided to meet him later at a party.

In retrospect, I'm not really sure why I even agreed to hook up with him. Probably somewhere in the back of my mind I knew there was something to him. This guy wasn't just some nappy-headed brother sending one of his homeboys to try and hook him up. I mean, my music professor had spent half the class raving about how this talented young musician was taking the world of music by storm. Everyone else in class was tripping all over themselves to get his autograph. So deep down, I knew I needed to check him out. And I let his interest feed right into my ego—of all the beautiful sisters on campus, this man had picked me.

So I met him at this party. And girl, the moment he looked into my eyes my heart started missing beats. After that first glance I was hooked. I don't know if it was his sexy voice or sense of humor or simply those beautiful baby browns, but I knew I had tripped over the edge. We connected instantly, powerfully, and way too fast. I was blown away by his electricity. We spent the whole night talking and laughing and relating. It was perfect. Then he was gone.

The next day he left for a European tour, but Mr. C., I am happy to report, kept in touch. He sent a couple of letters over the next few months and began calling me, playing sweet things on his instrument and charming me right down to my panties! Have you ever had a man play an instrument over the phone for you? It is *the* sexiest thing in the world. I developed a hunger for him that gnawed at me through classes and made it hard for me to concentrate. Finally, thank God, school let out and his European tour was over.

When he got home, we got together—at his posh apartment in New York. I found the music he made on stage wasn't the only type he could mold and slide right into your chest. That was merely a warm-up for the performance I got in the bedroom. That day and night we stayed indoors getting to know each other real well (if you know what I mean). We didn't even stop long enough to eat!

Okay, let me just explain something about myself. Before him, good sex for me had meant laying there quietly in missionary position pretending to be overtaken while the guy was on top doing all the work. He would climax. And that would be the end of story. Not this time. My man was a bedroom teacher. He took me to new heights. Redefined the use of a bathtub, girl. And proved sex was something that didn't only get hot after dark. Before it was over, I was the aggressor, guiding him to places where I would get the most pleasure. I even laughed while we tossed each other back and forth, and took turns on top. For me, sex had never been something during which you could laugh or talk. But my man made me laugh, pure and simple. I just couldn't take sex so seriously when

I was with him. No performance anxiety allowed. This was a fantasy come true. We were in sync—mind, body, and soul.

His fingers were magic. He played my body till I figured I had been made explicitly for him! After making love with this brother I could assist any corporation with their studies on sexuality. And remember I was a conservative young thing who believed that good girls don't do stuff like Mr. C. and I did. (I know you know what I'm talking about. You grew up with this belief, too.)

With Mr. C. I came to truly understand what a difference equal participation means. There is no way you can receive pleasure if mentally you have no business in bed with your partner. But if your man respects and genuinely cares about your feelings, you're in store for some awesome lovemaking.

I know what you're thinking. You're saying, "Wait, now was this only the second time they'd met?" Yes, all right, Smarty Pants. I decided to sleep with him only the second time we'd ever been together. And I had no guilt about it, Miss Thang. But just so you know, that *was* a personal record for me. So stop wrinkling your nose!

Because that first time was so wonderful, though, I had a scary attachment to this man. I did not want to leave him for one moment, forget an entire year for him to go back on tour. And I realized that when he got back, I'd be off studying abroad for the next two semesters. My heart broke that weekend when he said good-bye to me. (I still can't believe how emotional I was.) And he felt it, too. It was clear that the man wanted me. He was as captivated by me as I was by him. We even talked about marriage. But the bottom line was we hardly knew each other. We'd had a few magical days and nights, what more was there? My heart was torn. I wanted to end it. Knew I should end it. But I couldn't.

More than eight months passed before I heard from him again. By this time I had tried to forget him and was seeing someone else.

I was happy—until he called. He said he'd tried calling me but had never gotten through; he'd been out of the country; he had a million reasons why so much time had lapsed. But he'd never stopped thinking about me, he said, wanting me, and anticipating me. Right there on the telephone, thousands of miles away, he rekindled the magic we'd made and hooked me again, just as fast.

Almost without thinking, I dropped the guy I was dating and went back to Mr. C. This became the story of my life. In three years, we would be face-to-face less than half a dozen times. Yet in my heart and mind he became the single most influential love of my life.

It was unbelievable how much power he had over me. I still don't understand the intensity of my feelings for the man. This relationship, or more accurately, lack of relationship, consumed me. After a while, I stopped recognizing myself. I would drop anyone and everything the very second Mr. C wanted my attention. Whenever we were together, all the celebrity perks turned my life into a fairy tale—the limo rides, backstage passes, big houses, celebrity friends. We'd spend a day in splendor and a night in bed. Then he was off to God-only-knows-where for who-knows-how-long. I'd be left to suffer and reestablish my life in his absence, always anticipating a call from him.

I held on for dear life to the idea that, regardless of what I had to go through, in the end I would get my prince charming. Lovemaking, I reasoned, would be my magical remedy. The more sex I gave him, the more he would want me. If only I could re-create the magic, the emotions, and the attachment we shared during our first sexual encounter. Sex would be the way I would get him to stay around longer, come back sooner, and stop leaving me for his career. Unfortunately, each time we had sex—whenever he was in town—I felt less connected to him.

Something was wrong.

I got a glimmer of it when we had to plan a date that was five months away. We decided in October while he was away touring that we would meet in March when he would be performing in my city. I would attend one of his concerts and we would hook up afterward. I was so excited about finally seeing him that time flew by.

In March, I rounded up a few of my girlfriends and went strutting to the concert. By this time Mr. C was a huge celebrity, doing television, films, and music. He was making a name for himself when we first met, but tonight his star had never been brighter; he filled that huge concert hall to capacity—sold out all the seats in the place.

In the audience that night I felt so proud of him. I sat there thrilled to see all the shining faces moved by his music, connecting with the beauty and loveliness of his soul. I even sent a message back to his dressing room before the intermission to say hello and tell him how excited I was that we were finally going to be together.

After the concert, I went backstage, where we'd agreed to meet, and found that the security guards wouldn't let me through. Mr. C had forgotten to put me on the VIP guest list. His fan club line—so many little girls—was just too long—no way was I gonna wait for him among a bunch of groupies. My pride was too big at that point.

But my ego, to say the very least, was majorly bruised. He blew me off. *Me!* I refused to speak to him for three months after that concert.

You know, this man had always made me believe we had something special together. I knew his lifestyle took a huge chunk of him away, but whenever he looked into my eyes all that absence melted away. We could be *real* with each other. We could share parts of each other that we both didn't share with others.

I guess love and great sex blinds you to reality—the reality that everyone else can see so clearly.

After a while, it truly sunk in that Mr. C's world was too big to include me. When someone very dear to both of us passed away, he popped into my life for a brief interlude, a commercial break, and left to continue his thing without a second thought. I have to admit he was wonderful for about a month. He came and stayed with me and we both grieved and held each other up. But I guess he figured a month was adequate grieving time and soon left me to fend for myself. He stored his emotions away easily and suggested I do the same.

But I was emotionally shot and needed him for more than a month to be there for me. When I called him for support and love, he asked me not to badger him while he was touring. He told me he had to focus on his work and couldn't afford to be distracted.

Listen, when someone says they love you, but has no time for you, it really hurts. You know I'm a strong person, Cuz. But this was just too much for me. When I had to suffer that death alone, I finally opened my eyes.

I was tired, tired of the uncertainty, tired of feeling unloved by Mr. C (who had become a not-so-hot celebrity in my book) for most of the year. Yeah, he was sexy, and could wail on his horn, but I needed more than that. I was *worth* more than that. In time I gathered enough strength to end the whole affair. And believe me, it wasn't easy. I mean this man made my heart sing. But still, I couldn't be second fiddle to his celebrity lifestyle. The price I paid to be paraded around and treated like a princess was too high in the end, when I was left all alone, out of the spotlight—out of *his* spotlight—craving affection. I knew I needed to be first in this man's life—-or out of his life forever.

Girl, I'll never use my body to win someone's heart again. It's hard for me to believe that's where my thinking had gone. I gave him too much of myself—my body and my mind—in an attempt to keep him in love with me. And I do believe he loved me at one time. But he got too lost in the world of fame and fortune, especially during the most crucial times of our relationship.

Now that it's over, I will never again sacrifice my dreams to be held tightly by a man.

My celebrity didn't let anything get in the way of his career. That's probably why he is so famous. And that's why I came to understand that our relationship would never work.

Today is a new day for me, Cuz. I'm free to make good choices and to love myself. My heart belongs to *me* again—no more waiting around for Prince Charming to ride in on his horse whenever he feels like it.

Now I know that my experiences can empower me if only I look them straight in the face and put them firmly in the past. And I hope that you know it, too. Please, darling, don't make the same mistakes I made. (Smile—there you go, wrinkling your face again, accusing me of being a bossy older cousin.)

Okay, so I'll stop. At least we're up to date. Will you forgive me for not writing to you in so long? (Yeah, now *you're* smiling. You could never stay mad at me for too long.)

I figure we should begin sharing our stories more and more— all of our stories. Maybe then we won't hurt alone. Maybe then we won't even hurt at all because we're watching out for each other.

Well, that's my trip down celebrity lane. What's up on your side of the world?

Write me back, please. I love you!

Love,

Lisa

Breaking the Silence
by Kim-Monique Johnson

I used to date different guys, but no one seriously. All my friends had steady boyfriends and were having sex; I was the only "late bloomer." To my mother, I was doing the right thing by not becoming too attached to any one guy. Maybe she was living vicariously through me, her eldest, after having me at age eighteen, marrying my father at age twenty, and divorcing him a short time later.

"You sure pick 'em up and put 'em down, don't you, girl!" was my mother's favorite line about my short-lived relationships with guys. Mama encouraged me to go slow, to explore, to not rush into sex. And I took her advice to heart when I met my best friend Traci. I wasn't fully aware of it at the time, but my lesbian feelings began to stir the closer Traci and I grew.

We had both just ended relationships with guys and were taking a break from dating. Along with the intimacies of sharing our triumphs, disappointments, and aspirations, came physical intimacy. Not sexual, just very sensual. I would wash Traci's hair, she would massage my back; I would rub her feet, she would stroke my head. With each tease we approached a fine line between massage and caress, between touching and fondling. But we dared not speak on it. Neither one of us had ever made love to a girl before and we could only secretly fantasize about being each other's first lesbian love. That intensified the desire.

At each stolen moment I asked myself, *Is this lesbianism?* Maybe I would have understood better if I'd known even one black gay woman. But the only gay people I knew of were white men. And I had only negative stereotypes and myths of lesbians and gays. I didn't think I was anything like a *real* lesbian. I assumed all lesbians were boyish women who only wore boots and Birkenstock sandals, and owned toolboxes. Even with my shaved head, which I sometimes wore underneath a bandanna, I thought I was too feminine for dykedom. Besides, I figured I couldn't be gay because, at that point, I hadn't actually had sex with Traci, I'd only fantasized about it.

I convinced myself that it wasn't being gay that made me glow inside every time Traci and I touched; it was simply the taboo that made it so intensely erotic. Then, one summer, a heat wave hit New York, and we finally became lovers.

One night, when Traci slept over, I casually said, "Heat rises, so let's sleep on the floor." I had only enough cushion to assure our bodies would be close. Traci accepted my corny invitation and agreed to sleep on the floor next to me. I really wanted her in my bed but I couldn't think of a good line to get her there. She must have known I was trying to get as close as I could to her, but she didn't let on. Her hands felt so soft as we began our usual mutual caressing. The charge was so strong that the passion was almost painful. I dove headfirst into the softness of her face. Kissing and holding her felt so familiar—there was nothing foreign or unnatural about it. I marveled at the uniqueness within our sameness. Making love to her was like making love to myself; it was a glorious affirmation of who I was becoming.

This went on for two years. I could accept my love for Traci yet I still couldn't accept myself as a lesbian. I wasn't ready for what I thought would be adopting a certain "lifestyle"—hangin' out in gay bars where people smoke and drink too much, and parading bare-breasted on subways and city streets. Instead I lived as a closet lesbian—closeted even to myself—while I waited for the right guy to come along so I could live heterosexually ever after. But that never happened.

Eventually I found a support group for lesbian and bisexual women of color. I attended poetry readings and book signings sponsored by and for women, read about black lesbian and gay communities, both in the United States and throughout the African Diaspora, and received guidance from a woman who was black and bisexual.

Although I gained a better understanding of what my gayness meant for me, I was still hiding it because no one close to me knew. But that's when the unexpected happened.

One day, my sister and I were hanging out in her room. She was packing away some clothes and I was playing with her three-month-old baby girl, my godchild.

"Kim, can I ask you something?" my sister began. My heart skipped a beat at the seriousness in her voice, yet I certainly wasn't prepared for her next question.

"The other day the door to your room was open and I over-heard a woman leave a detailed message on your answering machine about the time you two spent together." Short pause and then, "Are you gay?"

Oh no, I thought—*confronted.* I felt exposed and vulnerable, then angry at myself for forgetting to turn down the volume on my answering machine. I picked up my niece and held her close, as I began to cry.

"Yes," I squeaked. With my voice still shaking I asked, "Does this mean you don't want me to be Jewel's godmother anymore?"

"*What?*" My sister looked embarrassed. "*No!*" she said. "I didn't mean to make you cry. Maybe I shouldn't have asked, but it doesn't matter to me *what* you are, you're my sister, and I love you."

Even though it wasn't by my own doing, I was relieved to finally be out to someone in my family. My sister has always been easygoing and nonjudgmental and our talk gave me the resolve to tell my mother. I didn't want Mama to also find out by accident. More importantly, I wanted her to hear it from me. Based on my reaction to my sister asking me about my sexuality, I realized I was not as comfortable with coming out as I wanted to believe. I had built up a family of outside supports for myself, but now it was time to be real with my blood family.

Several days later I told my mother. I was scared, but I reminded myself of my mother's openness and her constant encouragement for me to live life fully.

"Ma, I have something to tell you," I said abruptly.

"You're pregnant!" She jumped in with wide eyes.

"No." I smiled back.

"You're running away to get married?" she asked. I really laughed then. The irony was making for a great coming-out story.

"No, I told you Steve and I aren't together anymore."

"What then—your brother's pregnant? His girlfriend's having a baby, I mean . . . ?" Her worry made me wonder, *What would be easier for her to hear? That my troubled, unemployed nineteen-year-old brother is becoming a father, or that her daughter is a lesbian?* At that moment I hoped that my news would be easier for her to take. So, I plunged right in.

"Ma, this is about *me*. I want you to know before you find out by accident." I took off my glasses and rubbed my eyes. This was my way of dealing with my nervousness while playing it off as being cool. And with my extreme near-sightedness, I could tell Mama the truth while looking her straight in the eye, without ever seeing her face.

"I get my deepest connection and emotional support from other women, from close sister-friends. It's the real reason why I'm not with Steve anymore." I didn't have to see Mama's face to know she understood what I meant.

"You're *gay*?" she asked.

"Yes, Ma, I'm gay."

Mama slowly rubbed her palms on her lap. Quietly she asked, "Is it Traci?"

I put my glasses back on. "Yes," I answered, "but how did you know?"

"Well, you two have been so close for so long."

I nodded agreement.

Taking a deep breath, Mama said, "Well, I'll tell you something, and this may sound crazy. But I wish I had a close sister-friend. Someone to talk to, I mean, to get support from. It seems like I'm always looking for a man to give me what I need, and I haven't found it yet. We black women have got to stop relying solely on these men to make us happy. We've got to uplift each other and depend on one another, no matter what. Whether you're straight or gay, I don't care, just make sure you know how to make *yourself* happy. Are you happy, Kim?"

I nodded again, as joyous tears welled in my eyes. She went on, "I love you. And tell Traci I love her, too."

Fortified with my family's acceptance I let go of my fears of being confronted and "outed." I learned that the things I feared most often don't happen anyway. I'm fully out now, not just from the "closet" but also from underneath the stigma that engulfed me. The only things I lost were my ignorant stereotypes, and my homophobia. Once I proclaimed my lesbianism I didn't suddenly start drinking or smoking, or wearing boots. Nor did I come home and find all my dresses and skirts replaced with baggy jeans and plaid shirts. I did, however, buy myself a toolbox so that I'd be prepared when things needed fixing. Being gay wasn't about being thrown into a "lifestyle" that was any different from the one I had been leading all along. I was already in the life I had been so afraid to own. I was living life just being me, a gay black woman.

Today my life is about making new friends and enjoying the company of women—all of them black and beautiful—who identify themselves as everything from "super femme" to "stone butch" (whatever those labels really mean). Now, my life's also about self-acceptance and coming out to my friends, one of whom surprised me by coming out to me in return!

Coming out to my mother gave me more than I had hoped. We have much more intimate conversations now and as a result of our newfound closeness, my mother is questioning the implications of her relationships with men and the women in her life. And in the same spirit, Mama's checking out her interactions with other black women.

As a black gay woman I take risks every day, just by being myself in a world that does not always want me to know I exist. Yet, whenever fear tries to silence me, I remember the words of poet Audre Lorde: if one black woman gains hope and strength from the realization that she is not alone, then it's well worth the risk of breaking the silence.

Moved to Strength

by Taiia Sojourner Smart

The bathroom was spinning like a crazed merry-go-round. The solid floor offered comfort to my bare feet, but none to my churning stomach. It felt like there was an alien trying to escape my body, but somehow it kept getting stuck in my throat. I knelt over the toilet, put one hand on the wall, and wrapped my arm around my waist like a seat belt. After three attempts, vomit finally bulldozed its way out, and I wearily flushed it down the toilet.

I stumbled back to my room and searched for the calendar I used to track my periods. Reluctantly, I flipped through the calendar pages praying to see the red X indicating October's monthly. But there was no X. I was late.

I peeked into my T-shirt and stared down at my breasts, swollen like melons. For weeks, they hadn't fit in any bra I owned. Why didn't I notice how tender they were before? Maybe I did notice but refused to believe that I could be pregnant.

How did this happen to me? Shateek and I used condoms. We were careful, weren't we? Then my mind raced back to the last time Shateek and I made love. We had ignored the broken condom, foolishly relying on the spermicide as our safety net.

I was pregnant. There was no doubt in my mind. That night, I called Shateek to discuss the change a baby would bring to our lives. I was selfishly worried about my future, and I knew that if I chose motherhood Shateek could opt to be a rolling stone, but I would have to be the Rock of Gibralter. My mind raced with scary questions, some of which I could already answer: Would Shateek support me if I kept the baby? Would he hate me if I didn't? Would I be able to finish school if I were to become a mother?

When Shateek and I talked about these things, I rambled on about how it was *my* body. I rattled off statistics I'd read in the newspaper about single mothers. While I spoke, Shateek was silent. What I took to be deep thought on his part, I later discovered was his fear. He groped for neutral words that wouldn't hurt me, mostly because I think he was at a loss for words. "Whatever you do I support your decision," he said.

"*Decision?* I haven't made a decision, yet. I just need some understanding."

But Shateek couldn't understand—at least not fully. I needed to talk to someone who knew my confusion. Confiding in the school nurse or a teacher were not options. One of my teachers was notorious for scolding mothers-to-be about throwing their lives away. She thought "smart" girls didn't have sex, and those who did were smart enough not to get pregnant.

Abortion wasn't a dirty little secret at school, it was more like an inevitable rite of passage, similar to menstruation. Those who didn't abort belonged to a kind of sorority of young single mothers. Their identifying symbols were their diaper bags and strollers.

I thought about calling my mother but quickly decided against it. Her words of caution from the time I was a young girl sounded in my ears: "Don't let those boys spoil you." My mother, like most mothers, hoped I would save my then teenaged body for marriage. She had been a teenage mother, and didn't want me to have to face the same struggles she had. But despite her good intentions, her advice couldn't quench the sexual fire that torched the veins of my blossoming body.

Although she knew I threw my virginity away years ago, I wasn't going to tell her I was pregnant. I'd disappointed her in the past by choosing thug-life boyfriends and sneaking out of the house, but those were signs of "growing pains" that couldn't compare to this.

During weeks of morning sickness, involuntary naps, and quarts of chocolate ice cream, I weighed the pros and cons of young unwed motherhood. I knew I wasn't mentally, spiritually, or financially prepared to raise a child. I refused to add another digit to the list of statistics about black unwed mothers.

Eight weeks into my pregnancy, a sister-friend, Jill, drove me to the clinic. Ironically, in less than three months she would bring a life into this world and in less than three hours I would end one. As soon as Jill turned into the parking lot the car was mobbed by an angry group of pro-lifers. It was only seven o'clock in the morning and these people were shouting insults at us. Or were their jeers directly aimed at *me*?

Two clinic employees steered the group back to their legal protesting limits as Jill parked the car. One woman darted past the employees and slammed a picture of a fetus on the windshield and screamed, "You're a killer!" That was the worst hurt of all. I was about to take one of the hardest actions of my life, and somebody was calling me a murderer.

Inside the clinic, a nurse handed me the necessary paperwork—"standard clinic procedure." At the bottom of the page the bold print read, THE PATIENT GIVES THE DOCTOR THE PRIVILEGE NOT TO ADMINISTER THE ABORTION IF SHE IS UNCOOPERATIVE. Immediately I was on alert. I needed their services, and the last thing I would ever do was be uncooperative. I quickly read the rest of the form, scribbled my signature, and checked the "no" box requesting anesthesia.

Then came the doctor. He barely introduced himself when he shoved a gloved finger into my vagina. I was scared and uncertain, and my vaginal walls contracted against the pressure of his probing finger. *"Please, it hurts!"* I said through a shortened breath. But the doctor ignored me and continued his rough inspection. I jerked forward, yanked my feet from the stirrups, and stared into his icy blue eyes. He callously said, "Be still. This *doesn't* hurt. The sooner I get going, the sooner it will end."

He kept on jabbing at the center of my discomfort. I jerked forward again, this time pleading with my eyes for gentle treatment. When I refused to be silently abused, the doctor dismissed me as "uncooperative." As if I was invisible, he turned to the nurse and said, "She's not welcome here until she acts right."

I knew the difference between "standard clinic procedure" and deliberate harm. My gut triggered alarm and prompted me to leave the clinic, before my uterus ended up in a trash can. I had no intention of coming back. I needed the doctor's expertise, but I wasn't desperate for it. I deserved better treatment.

As fast as I could, I got dressed and left that place with a full refund and my African pride still intact.

Jill had gone home, and was coming to pick me up later. Clinic rules said family and friends couldn't stay and wait in the reception area. So there I was, all alone—pregnant, unmarried, and in need of help. I cried uncontrollably, like a child left alone in the dark. I knew there was only one person who could help make things feel better: I headed outside to the pay phone to call my mother.

I had been crazy to think I could go through this without her. Sure, we'd had our ups and downs. And, yeah, Mom had warned me about letting go of my virginity too soon. But all that didn't matter now. All I knew was that I needed the special comfort that only a mother can give when bandaging her daughter's wounds.

I dialed Mom's number slowly. When she answered, she knew it was me, almost before I spoke. Right away Mom told me that fish had haunted her dreams (an old superstition), and she knew I was pregnant. I expected disappointment, mixed with anger, but Mom's voice was encouraging, soothing, like the day she showed me how to cross the street when I was a little girl.

She told me that when she was pregnant with me, she was faced with the same fears and doubts about having a child. Then, treating me like the adult I had become, Mom asked straight out, "Do you want to keep the baby?"

Standing there at the busy pay phone, I weakened, swayed by the feel-good power babies have. I knew from watching my friends who were young mothers that at first babies smile in your face and cloud your thinking with worry-free fantasies. Then reality barges in, replacing those fantasies with bills and the education you put on hold; and you begin to wonder what really happens to a dream deferred? Mom and I spoke a bit more, her gentle voice soothing my uncertainty, and I knew what I had to do.

Three days later, with Mom's help, I found a caring woman doctor, and terminated my pregnancy. After it was over, I buried myself under the covers expecting guilt and shame to give me a life sentence of depression and regret. For two days I was awash with feelings—shame, disappointment, remorse—but the one feeling that kept rising to the surface over and over again was relief.

It's been a year and what I still feel is relief. I'm not depressed and I have no regrets. Looking back, I'm thankful that Roe vs. Wade helped legalize abortion, so that I wouldn't have to suffer at the hands of "back alley butchers" as so many women from my own family and neighborhood have done. I'm thankful that I have the power to control my body and to make choices that are best for me. Taking time to be alone, to reflect on what I've chosen, and why I'd done it, helped me feel good about my choice.

Months later, Shateek finally admitted he wasn't ready to be a parent and was pleased that he didn't have to take a crash course in fatherhood.

Pro-lifers think women who have abortions are heartless. But I look upon my abortion as a means of saving my life, and that takes the heart of a lion. My right to choose is a precious gift. The decision to end my pregnancy was a well-thought and selfless resolution. It's one of many chapters in my life in which my well-being hinged on an intelligent decision. I will continue to grow from this experience, and now I will take *all* the necessary precautions of a young woman in love.

Sometimes, when I watch proud mothers holding newborns at their breasts, and brown-skinned girls jumping double-Dutch in the park, my mind plays cruel tricks on me, nagging and cursing me for throwing away my unborn child. I'm easily coaxed into wondering who that child would have been. If she had been born, would she have had her daddy's almond-shaped eyes and my infectious smile?

Then questions of reality seep in. Would it have been fair to subject a baby to a cramped two-bedroom apartment with my sister and mother? Would that child have benefited from a mother who was forced to drop out of school? Would I have done right by my baby by having her at a time when I wasn't financially secure?

These questions, and their answers, assure me that I've made the right decision, that I've been moved to strength. I trust that I'll have a child when I'm better equipped to love, feed, clothe, protect, and teach her about her rights—especially the precious right to choose.

Quilt of Comfort

by Chemin Abner-Ware

*I will never leave you nor forsake you. . . . Lo, I will be with you
always even until the end of the world.*
Hebrews 13:5; Matthew 28:20

I had it all. In school I was one of the popular girls. I was the
best dancer, who everyone envied at the prom. I worked as a
model. And to top it all off, I was in love and in a committed
relationship with a rich, well-known guy. I was living the good
life—or so I thought.

I knew AIDS existed, but I didn't know anything about it.
Why should I? In my opinion, it was a disease that affected poor
people, homosexuals, and drug abusers. I never really thought
AIDS could apply to me—to the girl everybody liked, the pretty
one. AIDS was for other people, people with no money, the down-
and-out.

Well, when I was first diagnosed as HIV-positive over a
decade ago, my attitude about AIDS changed. And now that my
HIV diagnosis has turned into full-blown AIDS, I really look
upon the illness and those who have it much differently.

*And we know that all things work together for good to them that
love God, to them who are the called according to his purpose.*
Romans 8:28

It all started innocently enough. One night my sister and I went to a dance club on Rush Street in Chicago. We were just in a mood to party and be a little wild. So we drove to this swanky club. Two very fine older men approached and flirted with us throughout the evening. Even though I didn't let on, one of them caught my eye. He was tall, handsome, articulate, rich, famous, and twenty years older than I was.

I was in awe of him, and very attracted to the aura of confidence that surrounded him. But I played hard to get that night. I gave his friend my phone number instead of giving it directly to him, then we parted. To my surprise and delight, the guy I'd had my eye on called and asked to see me. We started a beautiful relationship. I thought I was in heaven. I felt so protected by him because he gave me a sense of security I never received from anyone, not even my own father.

Right away I saw that this guy would do the two things I desperately craved: he would love me and take care of me. My father hadn't been very supportive of me emotionally. He left when I was three years old. And became nothing more than a paycheck.

Even though my father was not there for me, I still wanted to be Daddy's little girl, to have Daddy sweep in and solve my problems. But deep down I knew that would never happen. So I guess I looked for "Daddy" in the people I dated. That's why this guy seemed like such a godsend.

He wasn't my first boyfriend, but he was the one who would change my life forever. Before him, I never really enjoyed sex much. I lost my virginity at a motel when I was sixteen and did not like sex then or for years to follow. I always thought it was something I was supposed to do to please the men in my life and then they would care for me emotionally and spiritually. I fell for lines that never rang completely true. "Baby, I just want to show you how much I love you." "If you love me, you will do it." I listened to the most pathetic, manipulative lines and opened my rigid body to their lies.

But this man was different. He was sensitive and compassionate. We had a *great* time for a year. Then slowly the joy seeped out of our relationship. He became verbally abusive and started drinking constantly. Once, he lost twenty pounds within two weeks and was hospitalized for a liver breakdown. But I never suspected anything was seriously wrong with him. He complained constantly of colds and suffered from cold sweats, but I figured alcohol and a bad attitude caused his problems.

Again, AIDS to me was something *other* people contracted, so it didn't ever occur to me that my boyfriend could have the virus. I never thought a well-educated, smart man could get it. Even when I felt swollen lymph glands in my own throat that prevented me from eating and swallowing, I never thought it could be a fatal disease. Even when I felt tired all the time and had become susceptible to cold sweats, or when the lymph glands under my arms were swollen, I thought my body was just reacting to the stress this man had placed in my lap.

I broke up with him after a year and moved on with my life. Two years later, I met a fabulous guy who eventually became my husband. This man was healthy and treated me with respect and kindness, and I came to realize that he was really the person I was meant to be with.

Life was good again—whole. Then soon rumors surrounding my ex began to fly. People were saying he was in the hospital with AIDS. Oh, no. That had to be a malicious lie, right? My soon-to-be-husband and I were scheduled to fly to Las Vegas and tie the knot, but I couldn't get married with that hanging over my head. So I phoned my ex and asked him point blank whether he had AIDS. And he said, "No, absolutely not. The rumors are all lies." Okay. So I left and got married.

Three months later, an old friend of mine called to say that a mutual friend had attempted suicide because she had the AIDS virus. That hit me hard, not only because of her despair and pain, but because the woman, according to my friend, had contracted the disease from my ex. I went into shock. It was, after all, only three months into my marriage. Something about what my friend was proposing held true. I wondered, Why would she call me and tell me about AIDS, if it *weren't* true? If it was a joke, it was a cruel joke. But the veracity of her words made me truly consider AIDS: the cold sweats, the lymph glands . . . it was beginning to make sense.

I knew I had to get tested. So the next day my husband and I went to the testing site together. When we finally got the results, I was neither stunned nor shocked when my test came back positive. *HIV positive.* The words rang through me as if they were from another dimension. I kept thinking I'd wake up and it would all be over. My ex had lied. That man had played with my life. A couple of weeks later he died.

I went on to finish out that semester of school, like nothing had happened. For almost a year, my husband and I didn't really talk about my positive test results. We didn't use condoms religiously and I refused to go on the antiviral drug AZT, which slows the spread of the virus in individuals. Only my husband and I knew about my health, and he stood by my side faithfully. He went to all my doctor appointments with me, held me when I cried at night, and explained to me that God was not punishing me with the virus. That God loved me no matter what. But still, we were both in denial about the illness.

After time and time again of unsafe sex, I got pregnant—something that was supposed to be a blessing to a marriage, was, for us, a big mistake. I knew I couldn't give a child my disease or bring a child into this world who would more likely than not grow up without its mother. I had an abortion, got a tubal ligation to prevent future pregnancies, and truly began facing the reality of my illness.

My husband and I became responsible sexually, always using a condom. And my husband got tested. Fortunately, he tested negative. We had a wonderful life, a fabulous restaurant, a beautiful loft, and then, one day it was gone. The house, the restaurant, and our whole life was taken from us—HIV and then eviction. The stress of the disease began to take its toll on our marriage. We began the stroll down the aisle of divorce court.

Soon after, I told my family that I was HIV positive. That was the best thing I could have done. Like a warm quilt of comfort wrapping its fabric of love around me, my family supported me beyond my wildest dreams.

I was waitressing and modeling at that time, and I remember telling my mother about my disease over the phone. She took the bus across town to my job, and, with tears in her eyes, hugged me and said she loved me. My mother had never taken public transportation before in her life. What may seem like a small action—riding a city bus—was an outpouring of love on her part.

When I told my sister, Diane, about my HIV, she wept. Her heart was broken. She told me she'd dreamt she had contracted a terminal illness, and, in the dream, felt relieved that of all the people in the family it had happened to her. When, in real life, she discovered it was actually her baby sister who had the fatal disease, she was right there for me. Diane has always been solid in her faith in God, and she told me He would help us get through this. She kept me emotionally and spiritually sound with Bible scriptures, and she stopped me from entering the great dark void that had begun to engulf me. I attended a Bible study class one evening and sat in a trance listening as the reverend taught The Word. I finally realized Jesus was the older man I'd been looking for all my life. He was the loving Father who had come to love and deliver me from all that felt so empty.

On that night, I felt like I had been cleansed—all my sins washed away. All was forgiven.

Therefore if any man be in Christ, he is a new creature: old things are passed away; behold, all things are become new.
II Corinthians 5:17

AIDS has no conscience. It steals and destroys life. Any life. It has no preference to age, race, or financial status. I take approximately fourteen pills a day. I still weigh my normal weight; in fact I've even gained ten pounds because of the medicine. But waking up in the morning is extremely difficult. Simple tasks like dressing or doing my hair zap all the energy and strength from me. I am constantly sleepy. I had to stop modeling because of my extreme fatigue and inability to travel. It became impossible to explain my lack of energy and constant colds to my modeling agency. My husband and I patched up our differences, but he remains at risk for catching the virus every time we engage in sex. My vaginal fluids can seep out and make contact with his, or the condom could be faulty. The only real chance of him not getting the disease is for us to abstain from sex.

The virus stole the joy out of my life, but it hasn't taken my spirit. My body may not hold out much longer, but I know *I* will survive. It's been a long journey to this point, a journey of faith and light and trust.

I used to spend my time contemplating suicide. I would lay in my bed and plan on walking in front of cars, or overdosing on cough medicine or sleeping pills. But with the help of my sister, Diane, God's voice has come through the fog. One evening, the voice said to me that there was refuge and strength right inside myself—that I should stand up and *live*. And the voice keeps on, keeps telling me to look ahead, not backward. To look up, not down. Now, the only thing I want to put to rest are my burdens, and when I have a moment of feeling low, I simply lay my troubles in God's hands. I've been doing that a lot these days, and it's allowed me to come to a place of peace in my soul about the virus.

Unless an inexpensive cure is discovered, I will surely die. My T-cells—the blood cells that fight off disease—are dropping, and I am at great risk of infection.

But I'm not bitter. I've overcome the anger I once felt for my ex-boyfriend. And I don't waste my precious time raging at his deceit. Actually, I feel sad for him.

In many respects, I still have it all: friends who love me, a family who hugs me whenever I need it, and a devoted husband who still stands by my side. And yes, I'm still a beautiful person—and rich beyond belief. You may never see my face on the cover of a magazine. But my healthy, brilliant spirit is what makes me a woman who is lovely to behold, a woman who is basking in wealth. I finally know that love is not sex, that I can honor my life, my body, and myself. Love is shown in how we care and cherish one another.

By the grace of God I know that there has been a purpose to my life, if only to help others who are living with AIDS. I will continue my work and the fight for my life until the Lord calls me home, then I will be cradled in the love and strength of His gentle arms.

Loving Arms
by Calinda N. Lee

It's 3:00 A.M. and I'm lying here—feeling his strong arms around me. I panic because they feel so good, and now that I have them, I don't ever want to lose them. I don't ever want to be afraid of a touch again, to be revolted by a caress in the dark. I promise myself for the millionth time that never again will I have to close my eyes and worry about being asleep, or fear fingers invading me.

Though I make this self-promise over and over, I can't escape the ugly memories. They're everywhere I turn. The horror of knowing that I am an incest survivor has filled me with shame. The hardest part has been living with this sickening secret.

Yeah, it's 3:00 A.M. and I feel my boyfriend Sekou's strong arms around me. His body is pressed to mine. His breaths are deep and slow. He's sleeping soundly; he won't budge. But I've been restless all night, tossing and turning. I can't stand being alone in this dark space. I wish Sekou would come out of his sleep and distract me for a while.

Finally, I try to wake him up. "Sekou, are you asleep?" I give him a nudge.

"Not anymore," he says. "What's wrong?" he asks gently.

Sekou's question confuses me.

"I don't know," I say. "I don't know what's wrong with me."

"Are you having another nightmare?" he asks.

I say, "Yeah, hold me please."

But Sekou already is holding me.

Soon the memories are fully stirred, and rather than being in bed with Sekou, I'm back to the days and nights of being a little girl. Papa is in the room and it's so late. *Why is he here?* I ask myself. *Did I forget to wipe off the stove, sweep the floor? Am I supposed to get up and do it?* But, really, I know better. I know why Papa's come.

He's moving slowly, too quietly—he's not supposed to be here. He's sneaking. *Play possum. Don't move; maybe he'll go away.* But my legs are being spread. *Be still, freeze—don't let him.*

But how can I stop Papa and pretend to be asleep, all at the same time? *Oh, God, please help me.* His hands are in my panties— *don't cry.* He's squeezing my nipples—*be still.* Back to my vagina— *don't scream—he'll know you're awake.* Then, before I know it, he's gone. Where did he go? Will he come back? I inch closer to my little sister in bed and put her arms around me, trying to find comfort in a safe embrace.

Next morning, I can't believe it's already time to get up and go to school. Mommy's impatient. "Why are you moving so slow, Calinda? Hurry up," she scolds. "As usual, you really have an attitude problem," she says.

Here we go again. I know the drill. Mommy's always getting on me about my "attitude." She insists that I'm always feeling sorry for myself. I want to tell Mommy what's going on. But will she believe me? Will she be on my side?

Papa's standing there, watching. His eyes bore into me. I know that look: *Get dressed, go to school, don't tell.* His gaze is so strong. No, I can never tell Mommy.

Hours later I'm in the girls' room, leaning against cold porcelain—*finally* crying, arms by my side because it disgusts me to touch myself. If I knew how, I'd hold me, I'd whisper *it's not your fault, Calinda*. But I'm too ashamed. I keep my arms by my side.

Back with Sekou, I'm so scared. Why am I seeing these pictures from so long ago? It's ten years later. Sekou loves me; he won't hurt me. He'll keep those sweet, strong, caramel-colored arms around me for as long as I'd like.

Days later, sitting in my therapist's office, I can't breathe. I feel incredibly small sinking into the gigantic blue easy chair. Papa has come with me for a session. We're rehashing the past, those nights of invasion. He wrinkles his brow, announcing that he resents being villainized. He has so much control, even in my therapist's office. I really feel I'm losing the little power I've gained, since I've been getting help. Even my posture again resembles the posture of the little girl I was, apologizing for Papa's indiscretions. I fidget with my fingers, and suddenly become pigeon-toed, hunching my shoulders. "I'm not saying you're the villain, Papa," is all I can manage to mutter. As the session winds down, I ask myself, If Papa's not the bad guy, then who is?

For years I'm in psychiatric counseling. But the pastel walls and hushed tones of the therapy rooms fail to soothe my spirit. What *will* comfort me? I just don't know. With all this therapy, I feel as if I should have all the answers. *All* the answers.

But I don't. There's so much crying I still have to do. Some days it hurts so bad, I'm sure my chest will cave in and I will be crushed. I fear I'll choke and die on all my tears—years of tears. As time passes I just go limp and give myself over to exhaustion, crying in the shower. Weeping through my day at school. Whimpering in my bed, sometimes with Sekou, sometimes without him.

In time, the tears give way to anger, and I begin to rage in earnest for the child who was so wounded. And soon all the crying and praying, and finally *feeling* the pain, feels good, like it's saving me. It seems as if the hurting is healing me. And somehow, some way, I start to feel better. Slowly, I begin to turn to a few friends, an option I never considered before. Some become good friends— and I start to talk about what happened all those years ago.

In the months that follow, I stick close to the people I trust, to my girlfriends who really care about me.

In fact, many were people I never dreamed would care so much or so well about me. I come to think of them as my "angels"—honest, trustworthy souls. None of them hold the power to rescue me, yet collectively they begin to teach me the lessons I need to learn.

For years, I pretended nothing was wrong. I perfected the illusion of seeming fine. My angels point that out to me. Someone once told me that what I've been through must not have been so bad because I've always done so well in school, and I've always appeared so happy.

These friends, unexpected allies, show me many things about myself that I didn't know were true. And they teach me that I'm lovable, likable, that telling my truth won't drive everyone away. They teach me that no one deserves abuse and that I can find support from them when I need it.

Now my nights are different, better than before—less burdened by nightmares and bad memories. It's late and Sekou is visiting me. As usual, he wraps his strong arms around me. I can tell from his breathing that he's asleep, and I begin to cry—seriously sobbing, because I can really feel Sekou's arms, and I know they're not truly the arms I need, that it's my own caring touch that will heal me. *That's* the answer—all of it.

I gently push Sekou's arms away, so I am free to wrap my arms around myself. I rock myself to comfort while I lick the salty tears from my face. A smile spreads on my lips. I have never felt so secure, massaging the warm, beautiful skin of my shoulders. I promise myself a million times that I will never be afraid of a touch again. "I will protect you," I tell myself, meaning every word of this promise.

These arms feel so good, and now that I've found them, I don't ever want to lose them. I will never let them go.

Resource Directory

Resource Directory
Compiled by Joyce E. Davis

The stories in this book may encourage you to seek more information about your sexual health. The resources listed here can provide you with further knowledge. In some cases, only a telephone number is cited. On other listings there is no explanatory information on the resource's offerings. Every effort has been made to obtain complete information for each listing. Entries cited in bold have data directly relating to African Americans. There are also many caring people whom you know—family, friends, clergy—who may be able to offer you guidance.

ABORTION/BIRTH CONTROL/PREGNANCY

Toll-Free Resources

National Abortion Federation Hot Line
800-772-9100

National Association of Mother's Centers
336 Fulton Avenue
Hempstead, NY 11550
800-645-3825
516-486-6614 (in New York)
Provides research, advocacy, and support for those involved in parenting, pregnancy, childbirth, and child rearing.

Planned Parenthood National Headquarters
800-230-PLAN

Pregnancy Hot Line
800-238-4269

National Resources
Black Americans for Life
National Right To Life
419 7th Street NW, Suite 500
Washington, DC 20004
202-626-8800
Educates black community on pro-life and pro-family issues by supporting education, legislation, and political candidates who seek to protect those victimized by abortion.

Florence Crittenton Division of Child Welfare
League of America
440 First Street NW, Suite 310
Washington, DC 20001
202-638-2952
A national adolescent pregnancy service focusing on sexuality and self-esteem.

Local Resources
Heartbeat
2292 Olentangy River Road, Suite E
Columbus, OH 43227
614-885-7577
Provides referrals to local organizations and contacts for those seeking crisis pregnancy and postabortion help.

Teens Against Pre-Marital Sex (TAPS)
2828 Vernon Place
Cincinnati, OH 45219
513-569-8500 ext. 124

An abstinence program that sponsors retreats and after-school clubs for those who have made or want to make the decision to abstain from sex, drugs, and alcohol.

LESBIAN AND BISEXUAL
National Resources
Parents and Friends of Lesbians and Gays, Inc. (P-FLAG)
110 West 14th Street NW
Washington, DC 20005
202-638-4200

Offers help in strengthening families through parent support groups, educational outreach, newsletter, chapter development guidelines, family AIDS groups, advocacy, information, and referrals.

Local Resources
Arizona AIDS Information Line/Lesbian and Gay Community
602-234-2752

Gay and Lesbian Community Center of Baltimore (GLCCB)
241 West Chase Street
Baltimore, MD 21201
410-837-5445

Gay and Lesbian Youth in New Jersey (GALY-NJ)
PO Box 137
Convent Station, NJ 07961
201-285-1595

Gay & Lesbian Community Action Council (GLCAC)

310 East 38th Street

Minneapolis, MN 55409

612-822-0127

Council provides services to homosexual community in the form of a same-sex domestic violence program, information, referrals, and social services.

Gay Milwaukee Youth

Box 09441

Milwaukee, WI 53209

414-265-8500

Gay Youth Alliance

3916 Normal Street

San Diego, CA 92103

619-233-9309

Lesbian, Gay and Bisexual Student Union (LGBSU)

PO Box 65914

Tallahassee, FL 32313

904-644-8804

Lesbian, Bisexual and Gay Services of Kansas

Box 13, Kansas Union

Lawrence, KS 66045

913-864-3091

Lesbian and Gay Community Services Center
208 West 13th Street
New York, NY 10011
212-620-7310
The center has a subgroup that supports African American lesbians.

Our Own Place (OOP)
PO Box 25443
Durham, NC 27702
919-688-9966
Support for lesbian women.

The Pacific Center for Human Growth
2712 Telegraph Avenue
Berkeley, CA 94705
510-548-8283
510-841-6224 Sexual Minority Switchboard
510-548-2192 Counseling Request Line
Center provides services including HIV/AIDS testing and support groups, outreach services, and peer support for lesbians, gay men, bisexuals, transsexuals, and transvestites. Also provides counselors specifically trained to address issues concerning people of color.

Sexual Minority Youth Assistance League (SMYAL)
333 1/2 Pennsylvania Avenue SE
Washington, DC 20003-1148
202-546-5940
202-546-5911 Help Line
Provides support to gay and lesbian youth in the form of weekly support groups for those ages 14–21 and safe spaces for interaction with other gay and lesbian youth.

Sister II Sister

Gay, Lesbian and Bisexual Community Services

Center of Colorado

PO Drawer 18E

Denver, CO 80218-0140

303-831-6268

A support group for black lesbians.

Spectrum, Center for Lesbian, Gay and Bisexual Concerns

1000 Sir Francis Drake Boulevard, No. 12

San Anselmo, CA 94960

415-457-1115

Your Turf

PO Box 2094

Hartford, CT 06145

203-278-4163

A gay, lesbian, and bisexual youth group that offers many activities as well as support groups for youth under 21 through the Hartford Gay and Lesbian Health Collective.

SEXUAL ABUSE (RAPE/INCEST/MOLESTATION)

Toll-Free Resources

Delaware Rape Crisis

800-262-9800

Local Resources

Battered Women's Task Force

Domestic Violence and Sexual Assault Programs

YWCA, Topeka

225 SW 12th Street

Topeka, KS 66612

913-354-7927 Office

913-233-1730 Hot Line

Services provided include crisis intervention, shelter, counseling, support groups, and alternatives to battering.

Center Against Rape and Domestic Violence

PO Box 914

Corvallis, OR 97339

503-758-0219

541-754-0110 Hot Line

Center provides shelter, support groups for victims of sexual assault and domestic violence and referrals.

Center for Victims of Violent Crime (CVVC)

1520 Penn Avenue

Pittsburgh, PA 15222

412-392-8582

Center offers victim advocate services, youth intervention, and referrals for victims of sexual assault.

Connecticut Sexual Assault Crisis Services, Inc.

Call for one of 11 hot lines at the center nearest you.

203-282-9881

203-522-4636 Information Line

Crisis Intervention and Suicide Prevention
Center of San Mateo County
1860 El Camino, #400
Burlingame, CA 94010
415-692-6662
415-692-RAPE Rape Crisis Hot Line
Sponsors rape crisis service and group counseling for survivors of rape and perpetrators of domestic violence.

Daughters and Sons United
c/o Giarreto Institute
232 East Gish Road, 1st Floor
San Jose, CA 95112
408-453-7616
Counseling program for sexually abused children.

DeKalb Rape Crisis Assistance
PO Box 1291
Decatur, GA 30031
404-377-1428
Center provides 24-hour crisis line, in-house individual and group counseling for survivors and loved ones of rape victims.

The Friendship Center of Helena, Inc.
1503 Gallatin
Helena, MT 59601
Crisis Lines: 406-442-6800
800-248-3166
Center offers services including transitional shelter, counseling, battered women's support group, and a sexual assault outreach program.

Foothills Rape Crisis Center

PO Box 6264

Anderson, SC 29623

803-231-7273

800-585-8952 Hot Line

Offers short-term crisis counseling and advocacy, support groups, and Safe Touch programs.

Forbidden Zone Recovery

1580 Valencia

Suite 601

San Francisco, CA 94110

415-572-0571

For women sexually abused by professional men including therapists, MD's, clergy, attorneys, etc.

Incest Counseling Assistance Network

3549 North Sorrel

Northbrook, IL 60062-2230

Incest Resources, Inc.

46 Pleasant Street

Cambridge, MA 02139

Support for incest survivors and professionals working with survivors.

Incest Survivors Anonymous

PO Box 17245

Long Beach, CA 90807-7245

310-428-5599

Men, women, and teens meet to share their experience, strength, and hope, so they may recover from their incest experiences.

Pasadena-Foothill Valley Young Women's Christian Association (YWCA)

78 North Marengo Avenue

Pasadena, CA 91101

818-793-5171

818-793-3385 Hot Line

Operates 24-hour rape hot line and crisis center.

Pittsburgh Action Against Rape (PAAR)

81 South 19th Street

Pittsburgh, PA 15203

412-431-5665

412-765-2731 Hot Line

Offers medical and legal advocacy and crisis intervention counseling services to recent survivors of rape, attempted rape, sexual harassment and other forms of sexual violence.

Project Sister Sexual Assault & Prevention Crisis Services

PO Box 621

Claremont, CA 91711

909-623-1619

909-626-HELP Help Line

Provides information, referrals, counseling, support groups, and education and prevention services to those who have been affected by sexual assault.

Rape Action Committee
Women's Center
408 West Freeman
Carbondale, IL 62901
618-529-2324
Offers immediate advice and crisis intervention, medical and legal advocacy services, and counseling to sexual assault victims and significant others.

Rape and Sexual Abuse Center
56 Lindsley Avenue
Nashville, TN 37210
615-259-9055
Crisis Lines:
615-256-8526
800-879-1999 (only for Tennessee)
Offers support services to victims of sexual abuse.

Rape/Sexual Assault Group
Family Crisis Center
PO Box 1543
Great Bend, KS 67530
316-793-1965
For adult survivors of rape, sexual harassment, or child sexual abuse.

Seattle Rape Relief
1905 South Jackson
Seattle, WA 98144
206-325-5531
206-632-7273 Crisis Line
Offers crisis intervention and medical and legal advocacy for rape victims.

The Sex Abuse Treatment Center

1415 Kalakaua Avenue

Suite 201

Honolulu, HI 96826

808-973-8337

808-524-7273 Hot Line

Provides free medical, legal, educational, and emotional support to women, children, and their families who have been affected by sexual assault.

Sexual Assault Crisis Service

YWCA Hartford Program

135 Broad Street

Hartford, CT 06105

203-525-1163

860-522-6666 24-hour Hot Line

860-524-1182 Assistance/Counseling

Service offers counseling, support, and advocacy for victims of sexual violence including rape, incest, child sexual abuse, and sexual harassment. Services also offered for the victim's family, lovers, and friends.

Sexual Crisis Trauma Center of Greenville

25 Mills Avenue

Greenville, SC 29605

803-467-3633

Provides support groups for adult and adolescent survivors of incest and sexual abuse.

Society's League Against Molestation (SLAM) and Women Against Rape (WAR)

PO Box 346

Collingswood, NJ 08108

609-858-7800

SLAM provides general and legal information and referrals for those affected by child abuse. WAR provides telephone and in-house counseling for victims and their families and escorts for police, hospital, and court visits.

Survivors of Incest Anonymous

PO Box 21817

Baltimore, MD 21222-6817

Twelve-step program for persons 18 and up who have been victims of child sexual abuse and want to be survivors.

Voices in Action, Inc.

PO Box 148309

Chicago, IL 60614

312-327-1500

800-7-VOICE-A

Support for victims of incest and childhood sexual abuse.

Wichita Area Sexual Assault Center

215 North St. Francis

Suite 1

Wichita, KS 67202

316-263-0185

Offers programs for adolescent female victims (ages 13–17) of sexual assault. Also offers counseling for victims' family and friends.

Women Helping Women
PO Box 760
Paia, HI 96779
808-579-9581

Provides safe shelter and counseling for victims of family violence and rape/sexual assault.

Women Helping Women
216 East Ninth Street
Cincinnati, OH 45202
513-977-5541
513-381-5610 Crisis Line

Services provided to victims of incest, rape, and domestic violence include hospital and court advocacy and accompaniment, support groups, short-term intervention, and child sexual abuse and date rape prevention programs.

Women's Crisis Support Team
748 NW 5th Street
Grants Pass, OR 97526
503-479-9349

Team provides one-on-one counseling, support groups, and referrals and information to women in crisis.

Young Women's Christian Association of Oklahoma City (YWCA)
2460 NW 39th Street
Oklahoma City, OK 73112
405-948-1770

Sponsors program that focuses on domestic violence and rape.

SEXUALLY TRANSMITTED DISEASES

Toll-Free Resources

AIDS Clinical Trials Information Service
800-874-2572 (800-TRIALS-A)

AIDS Hot Line for Women
800-877-6013

Alabama AIDS Hot Line
800-228-0469

Center for Disease Control (CDC) National AIDS Hot Line
800-342-AIDS

Georgia AIDS Information Line
800-551-2728

National Sexually Transmitted Disease Hot Line
800-227-8922

Youth Only AIDS Line (not available in New York)
800-788-1234

National Resources

National Herpes Hot Line
919-361-8488

After AIDS Bereavement Support Group

PO Box 10488

Rochester, NY 14610

716-442-2220

Safe place of comfort, hope, and strength for anyone who has lost a loved one to AIDS.

AIDS Action Committee of Massachusetts

131 Clarendon Street

Boston, MA 02116

617-437-6200

Hot lines:

800-788-1234 (youth only; in Boston)

800-235-2331 (outside Boston)

Services offered include support group programs and individual therapy for people affected with HIV/AIDS, their friends, lovers, and families.

AIDS Foundation Houston, Inc.

3202 Weslayan/Annex

Houston, TX 77027

713-623-6796

Foundation provides services to those affected with HIV/AIDS in the form of individual and family case management, social service assistance, peer education, youth-at-risk programs, spiritual workshops, housing and financial assistance.

AIDS Project Hawaii
PO Box 8425
Honolulu, HI 96830
808-926-2122

Provides confidential support services to women and youth who are infected with or concerned about HIV/AIDS. Also provides support to friends and families.

American Institute for Teen AIDS Prevention, Inc.
PO Box 136116
Fort Worth, TX 76136
817-237-0230

Offers educational AIDS prevention programs for teens.

Arizona AIDS Project
115 E. Camelback Road
Phoenix, AZ 85012
602-265-3300

Services provided include case management, counseling, crisis intervention, hot line, support groups, and youth services.

Black Women's Health Council
PO Box 31089
Capital Heights, MD 20731
301-808-0786

Nonprofit organization serves the HIV/AIDS community of Price Georges County, MD. Free and confidential services offered include home visits, case management, spiritual/bereavement counseling, and nutrition support.

Brooklyn AIDS Task Force
465 Dean Street
Brooklyn, NY 11217
718-783-0883
800-293-3685

Services provided include community outreach and client intake, case management, extended family support services, lesbian and bisexual teen rap group, a pastoral care program, and a women's health program.

Cascade AIDS Project
620 SW Fifth Avenue
Portland, OR 97204
503-223-5907

Gainesville HELP (GHELP), Planned Parenthood
914 NW 13th Street
Gainesville, FL 32601
904-376-9000

Support for persons with herpes simplex virus.

Glide Goodlett HIV/AIDS Program
330 Ellis Street
Suite 518
San Francisco, CA 94102
415-775-3862

Offers free HIV testing, counseling, case management, drop-in support groups for all concerned with HIV and AIDS.

Herpes Resource Center
American Social Health Association
PO Box 13827
Research Triangle Park, NC 27709
919-361-8488 Hot Line
919-361-8400

Services offered include telephone network and support groups for persons with herpes.

Kansas City HELP (KCHELP)
PO Box 411694
Kansas City, MO 64141
913-599-9715 Herpes Hot Line

Confidential forum to exchange information, dispel myths, and support individuals dealing with physical and emotional aspects of herpes.

Knoxville HELP Group
5401 Kingston Pike
Suite 540
Knoxville, TN 37919
423-588-7598

Education, support, and assistance to adults with genital herpes.

Minority AIDS Outreach
2128 11th Avenue North
Nashville, TN 37208
615-391-3737

An AIDS education and prevention group that services the Nashville area.

NO/AIDS Task Force
1407 Decatur Street
New Orleans, LA 70116-2010
504-945-4000 Office
Hot lines:
800-99-AIDS-9 (outside New Orleans)
504-944-AIDS (in New Orleans)

Task force services include free HIV testing, early intervention services, case management, and outpatient clinic services. Offers information specifically for African Americans on HIV/AIDS. Multicultural Committee subgroup conducts education and outreach sessions in diverse communities.

Outreach, Inc.
3030 Campbellton Road, SW
Atlanta, GA 30311
404-349-4111

HIV/AIDS support groups, education, prevention, testing, counseling. Mom's Hands: mothers helping mothers with HIV/AIDS.

Regional AIDS Interfaith Network
504-523-3755 ext. 2917

Maintains a listing of priests, rabbis, and pastors who are supportive of HIV-positive people and their families.

Resources For Adolescents (RAP)
914 Richard Street
New Orleans, LA 70130
504-524-4611

RAP provides HIV-positive teens ages 13 to 19 with case management, support, and coordinated medical care, and offers prevention education for high-risk adolescent populations.

SisterLove Women's AIDS Project
1432 Donnelly Avenue, SW
Atlanta, GA 30310
404-753-7733
Provides support for African American women by women who are at risk for or are already infected with HIV or AIDS.

Tampa AIDS Network
11213 North Nebraska Avenue
Suite B-3
Tampa, FL 33612
813-979-1919 AIDS Info Resource Directory
Services offered include safer sex workshops, support groups for those affected by HIV/AIDS, case management, and individual, couple, and family counseling.

Tidewater AIDS Crisis Taskforce
9229 Granby Street, 2nd floor
Norfolk, VA 23503
804-583-1317
Offers education to prevent the spread of AIDS, case management, and volunteer and support services to those infected by HIV or AIDS.

Topeka AIDS Project
1915 SW Sixth Avenue
Topeka, KS 66606
913-232-3100
Support for people who are HIV positive and their significant others.

Unity Fellowship Church of Christ
Minority AIDS Project
5149 West Jefferson Blvd.
Los Angeles, CA 90016
213-936-4949

Women With a Vision, Inc.
704 N. Rampart Street, 2nd floor
New Orleans, LA 70116
504-524-1119
HIV education and prevention information, particularly for African American women.

WELLNESS/COUNSELING/SUPPORT SERVICES
Local Resources
Alaska Women's Resource Center
111 West 9th Avenue
Anchorage, AK 99501
907-276-0528
Center offers services including crisis intervention, counseling for women in abusive relationships, and pregnancy and health counseling.

Bebashi, Inc.
1233 Locust Street #401
Philadelphia, PA 19107-5414
215-546-4140
Education among the African American and Latino communities about sexual health issues, especially AIDS. Peer counseling, guest speakers, workers, and phone support.

Being Alive
111 E. Camelback Road
Phoenix, AZ 85012
602-265-4677

Services provided include counseling, crisis intervention, support groups, and youth services.

Caribbean Women's Health Association
2725 Church Avenue
Brooklyn, NY 11226
718-826-2942

Offers services on domestic violence, child abuse, HIV/AIDS, and referrals.

Center for Black Women's Wellness
National Black Women's Health Project
477 Windsor Street SW
Room 309
Atlanta, GA 30312
404-688-9202

Self-help programs, mammograms, pap smears, urinalysis, screening for STD, HIV, TB, AIDS, high blood pressure, vision and hearing, pregnancy.

Family Service of Philadelphia
718 Arch Street
Suite 304 South
Philadelphia, PA 19106
215-875-3300

Services offered include counseling on AIDS, domestic violence, dating violence, and teen pregnancy.

Feminist Women's Health Center
580 14th Street NW
Atlanta, GA 30318
404-875-7115
Pregnancy and STD/AIDS testing and counseling.

Haight Ashbury Free Clinics, Inc.
Women's Needs Center
1825 Haight Street
San Francisco, CA 94117
415-487-5619
415-487-5607 Clinic
Provides support to women in the form of medical services (gynecological care, pregnancy and HIV testing) and consultation and referrals for those who have been sexually abused.

Haitian Women's Program
464-466 Bergen Street
Brooklyn, NY 11217
718-399-0200
Services offered include domestic violence intervention, HIV peer education and training, adolescent AIDS education and HIV-positive case management to Haitian refugees and immigrants.

Turnabout Counseling
350 Virginia Avenue
Suite 1
Seaford, DE 19973
302-628-2011

Services provided include case management and support groups for those living with HIV and a resource center for youth under age 19 to prevent teen pregnancies, premature sexual activity, STDs, and HIV/AIDS through various types of counseling.

Women's Action Alliance
370 Lexington Avenue
Suite 603
New York, NY 10017
212-532-8330

Alliance provides programs in domestic violence, sexual harassment or abuse, prenatal care, nutrition, and maternal self-care. They also provide a resource listing for teenage pregnancy prevention programs.

Women's Resource and Action Center
The University of Iowa
130 North Madison Street
Iowa City, IA 52242
319-335-1486

Groups offered focus on issues including coming out, lesbian women discussions, sexual abuse/assault survival, lesbian alcoholism, incest survivors.

Authors' Biographies

Authors' Biographies

Tayari Jones's first name is a Swahili word meaning "she is prepared." She is a writer living in Houston, Texas, and teaches remedial reading at Prairie View A & M University, a historically black university outside of Houston.

Corliss Hill is the Lifestyle editor of *Essence* magazine. She holds a Bachelor of Arts degree in journalism and a certificate in African American studies from the University of Maryland at College Park. This native New Yorker also works as a freelance special events coordinator and publicist. She currently resides in Brooklyn.

Anasuya Isaacs has worked as a poet, actress, singer, playwright, television producer, translator, editor, teacher, and storyteller. At present, she is writing a feature-film screenplay and working as a finance administrator for a hospital in Brooklyn, New York, where she lives.

Eisa Nefertari Ulen is currently earning a Master of Arts degree in philosophy and education from Columbia University and has received a 1995 Frederick Douglass Creative Arts Center Fellowship to complete a collection of short stories. She has written for *Vibe, Shade,* the *City Sun,* and *Quarterly Black Review of Books.* She lives in New York City.

Lisa Chestnut-Chapman is a freelance writer, working on subjects that empower her community, especially black women. In addition, she volunteers for the Sudden Infant Death Syndrome Alliance. She lives in North Babylon, New York, with her daughter, Nicole, and son, Justin.

Kim-Monique Johnson serves as an HIV/AIDS program coordinator on Long Island, New York, and works as a freelance writer as well as a coproducer and cohost of a cable television talk show. She currently resides in Queens, New York.

Taiia Sojourner Smart has a Bachelor of Arts degree in communications from Johnson C. Smith University and currently works as an editorial assistant at *Essence* magazine. She lives in Brooklyn, New York, with her fiancé and plans to study magazine journalism at the graduate level.

Chemin Abner-Ware works with several programs based in her parish, the Salem Baptist Church, including the Big/Little Sister Foundation and Female Steppers for Christ. She also visits high schools and educates students about AIDS. She lives in Chicago.

Calinda N. Lee lives in Atlanta, Georgia, and has taught World Civilizations and the African Diaspora at Morehouse College and Spelman College, respectively, and is currently a member of the staff of the National Black Arts Festival. Her dedication to empowering women in this nation inspired her to share her personal experience in this book.

Joyce E. Davis is a writer living in Brooklyn, New York. She received a Bachelor of Arts degree in journalism from Howard University and is presently employed as a reporter at *Fortune* magazine, where she covers technology and medical business issues. She has also had articles published in *Essence, Vibe,* and *YSB* magazines.